A Fatal February in Edgemont

Second book in the Village of Edgemont cozy
mystery series

I0534424

Della North

A Fatal February in Edgemont

Village of Edgemont, Volume 2

Della North

Published by Lynda French, 2023.

A FATAL FEBRUARY IN EDGEMONT

First edition. September 30, 2023.

Copyright © 2023 Della North.

ISBN: 978-1998074075

Written by Della North.

A heartfelt thank you to Darlene Hartung for her wonderful encouragement, it means a lot.

Chapter One

Robert Wilcox knows this meeting isn't going to be pleasant, but he never imagined it will be fatal.

The retired Reverend, fondly known as Rev Robbie, arrives at the Edgemont Activity Centre with apprehension. As usual on a weekend, the parking lot is full but he has a reserved space in Staff Parking.

The weather is surprisingly mild for February in Alberta. Normally, a day like today with the clear blue sky, crisp air, and bright sunshine would have lifted the elderly man's spirits. But now, as the early winter darkness rolls in, he can't escape a strong feeling of foreboding.

He is facing up to a difficult task, an onerous duty, and the lighthearted greeting he receives from his visitor is disconcerting. It catches him off guard. Otherwise he might have survived because underneath his benign appearance Robert is an astute observer with no illusions about the darker side of human nature.

* * * * * *

Lila Morelli checks her medical bag to ensure the first aid kit is fully stocked. Her movements are mechanical and her mind is miles away. She's been wrapped up in her own unhappy thoughts for weeks now, and the misery she feels leaves her numb.

She has a problem but it isn't actually *her* problem, just as she has a secret that isn't *her* secret to keep or to tell. In every action she is simply going through the motions, her usual ebullience missing. She is in limbo.

However, she has schedules, deadlines, and obligations to meet. Like now, heading out to The Centre for a mixed league volleyball game. Lila isn't playing, she'll be on the bench in her capacity as volunteer nurse in case there is an injury on the court.

She's been attending the games for a few months and enjoys being involved except... well.. now she doesn't enjoy much of anything anymore. Drowning in unhappiness Lila carries her gloomy mood everywhere she goes.

* * * * * *

Last night had been special and so much fun. Judith Taylor and George Grant had driven out to the Banff townsite for what he'd called a *non-Valentine's February date.*

Both had enjoyed mingling with the upbeat crowd of tourists and skiers, everyone celebrating the season. The chill mountain air was fresh and clean.

After a dinner of back-ribs at Tony Roma's the two had wandered in and out of shops on the main drag. Stopping at a boutique confectioners Grant got chewy maple fudge and Judith had a gooey caramel chocolate for dessert. Then they drove to the Falls – which were half-frozen over – and followed the road to Surprise Corner where they admired the view of the Banff Springs Hotel all lit up like the castle it was styled after.

They were far enough away from Calgary's light pollution to witness what seemed to be a million stars in the sky. Looking up, trying to find and identify constellations, Grant had slipped his arm around Judith's shoulders and they both enjoyed the warmth that they felt inside and out.

Today, Judith is savouring the memory of a lovely night. Her friendship with Grant, which began so unexpectedly, is deepening in importance as well as intimacy.

They met when they'd been forced to work together because a flu bug decimated the administrative staff last year at Edgemont School for Girls while Grant was investigating the death of Holly Lezinsky, and the disappearance of Beth Penner, both students.

His unusual looks of very pale blond hair and ice-blue eyes made him a handsome man, but it was his gentle nature – despite his profession – that had attracted Judith the most. She feels scared, delighted, and intoxicated in anticipation of what the future will bring.

This evening she is joining Lila at The Centre to watch the volleyball tournament and have a final meeting with Rev Robbie. She's decided to take on the volunteer job of bookkeeper to free up more of his time. As a CPA Judith knows she'll have no difficulties with The Centre's books. It is a good cause with a friendly group of people, and Judith is experiencing the pleasure of helping out.

Chapter Two

Saturday, February 8, 2020

Eleanor and Basil Frampton were the driving force behind The Edgemont Activity Centre. They both spent a lot of time fundraising among their wealthy friends, and Basil served on the Board. When he passed away Eleanor took over his position.

Quite a large number of people call Edgemont Village home. Located in the foothills of the Canadian Rockies many types of people are attracted by its natural beauty.

The outer circle reside in a wide surrounding area on acreages, ranches, and hobby farms. The inner circle range from *comfortably off* in the Executive Estates enclave to the folks *getting by okay* in the trailer park. In between are bungalows and semi-detacheds, apartments and basement suites, townhouses and penthouses, with residents in all the tax brackets but mostly the top tier. Edgemont Village is home to wealth.

The land acquisition and building of The Centre, as it is known locally, was 100% donation-funded. At lot of money had poured in and what wasn't used in the building and hiring has been wisely invested.

Now that the Board includes an experienced grant-writer some government funding is coming in to promote specialty programmes. Originally geared towards sports The Centre now boasts Arts, Crafts, and Music classes.

A group of string musicians teach the Suzuki Method in bi-weekly lessons; there are drawing and painting classes for all ages; and visiting instructors give one-day demonstrations in activities such as painting on silk, researching your family tree, and photorealistic illustrating.

There's a Bridge Club; a Karate Club; several types of Yoga, Conversational French, Italian, German, and Chinese language classes; and lessons for all kinds of dance styles from tap to rap.

Patronage by the area's elite has made The Centre a worthy cause for its rich donors, and the volunteers enjoy a certain cachet from the association.

The Reverend Robert Wilcox's support increased after his retirement and when Peg, his beloved wife of almost fifty years died, his work at The Centre became the main focal point of his life. The short, and short-sighted, man with his fluff of white hair and cheerful smile is a familiar fixture.

As the little jobs he has taken on become big jobs he happily hands control over to younger volunteers, but he still oversees management of The Centre, and takes charge of the monies received each day.

Fees for the classes are usually processed online – which saves everyone a lot of time and bother – but earnings from the snack bar and donation boxes help build up the kitty.

The refreshment area sells canned soft drinks, coffees, and snacks – donated by local stores – and most of the visiting patrons will stuff a twenty or even a fifty into the cash-box by the front door. Edgemont Village is a retreat for the well-heeled and they are a generous bunch.

* * * * * *

Patricia and Mark Johnson are at The Centre attending an early Valentine's get-together of the Horticultural Society. They are both friendly, sociable people. Overweight – but not in a worrying way – with Pat's figure best described as *stately*. She's slightly taller than Mark but only because she always wears heels.

Other than an evening walk they don't exercise, but spend plenty of time outdoors happily working in their garden in the warm weather, and coaxing along their houseplants during the wintertime.

Pat is especially devoted to her African Violet collection, while Mark's interest lies mainly in the preservation of native plants. He is able to spend more time working with the Society now that he's retired.

The Society occasionally hosts guest speakers who bring slides to illustrate their talks, often accompanied by samples and cuttings. Most of their meetings are luncheons, but today is an evening event. Now, the members gather to enjoy decaf coffee and sweet nibbles catered from a local doughnut shop.

Pat plans to drop in on the volleyball tournament to lend support to the players from her school. She is the principal of Edgemont School for Girls and knows that several of her students will be playing, while some of her staff will be cheering them on. As usual, Mark is quite happy to socialize with their friends for the short time she'll be making an appearance in the auditorium.

* * * * * *

Detective George Grant and his partner, Suzanne Mirteau, are also at The Centre on this Saturday night checking the safety of the location before the visit of a couple of VIPs.

Some local bigwigs have fundraised enough to build an indoor skating rink. The ribbon-cutting ceremony is being performed by two holidaying minor Royals travelling the Trans-Canada Highway to ski at all the resorts from Banff National Park to Whistler, BC.

Their visit isn't happening until next month, in time for the Spring ski season, but protocol demands that all the arrangements be made, and the venues vetted by security professionals, well in advance of the event.

The two detectives make an eye-catching couple with her dark beauty offsetting his pale Nordic colouring. And as usual, they are arguing because they aren't a couple in the romantic sense and Suzanne is unable to accept that fact.

"Suzanne please, let's just finish off our checklist so we can leave. This day has already gone on forever and it's Saturday, I just want to go home and relax."

"Oh right, like I'm supposed to believe you don't have a hot date with your teacher or whatever she is."

"If you mean Judith Taylor she's the school bursar and, not that it's any of your business, we don't have a date tonight – hot or otherwise."

"Then you and I can go for a couple of drinks and discuss what we're going to have for breakfast," she says, flashing him a wicked grin that lights up her lovely face. Sparkling dark eyes, a cascade of wavy hair, and an athletic build always attracts the attention of all the men in her vicinity... except Grant.

When Suzanne flicks her tongue over her lips he doesn't see a sultry seductress but a narcissistic ego-driven control-freak. They've worked together for too long for Grant not to have encountered every aspect of Suzanne's nature. He's learned that beneath the beautiful looks she is bad-tempered, possessive, spiteful, and jealous.

With two divorces and quite a few bitterly ended romances all before the age of twenty-eight, Suzanne has grown more and more dissatisfied with her personal life. Grant, who had decided at the very start of his career not to get involved with coworkers, remains steadfastly immune to her charms – to her great annoyance.

Chapter Three

Saturday, February 8, 2020

Judith's pleasant thoughts of Grant end, and now her mind is dismayed over the troubles her co-worker Lila is enduring. Unfortunately there is very little Judith can do because Lila has thrown up barricades and refuses to explain.

Judith knows her friend's unhappiness has something – everything – to do with Arnie Chalmers, Lila's estranged husband. He'd flown out from Toronto at the New Year and Lila had been so excited that he was, finally, coming to see her, but whatever happened between the two of them wasn't good.

That's as much information as Lila is willing to give and Judith, afraid of damaging their new and valued friendship, doesn't push too hard. She will wait for Lila to confide and hopes it will happen soon.

The change in Lila is heartbreaking. Nothing seems to bring her out of her depression although Judith and Grant have tried, as have Beth Penner and her father Brian. Those two feel they owe a debt of gratitude to Lila for her support during Beth's ordeal in December.

Not too long ago Judith and Lila would have travelled to The Centre together, either from the school where they both work, or meeting at one or the other's home. After the game they'd have had a coffee and a gossip before returning to pick up whoever's car had been left behind.

When Judith suggests she drive them both tonight Lila has hurriedly said:

"No, I'll see you there," with no explanation.

Judith thinks back to her last visit to The Centre when she met with Rev Robbie to discuss her taking on the bookkeeping duties that he was finding too time-consuming.

"It's not that I mind the time I spend doing the work," he's told her, "but I sure resent the time I spend trying to find and fix my mistakes!"

He's a quiet-spoken jolly old man and Judith is very fond of him. Everyone thinks the world of Rev Robbie.

He isn't shy about asking when he wants something as Judith discovers at their recent meeting. He's come right out and asked her why she hasn't made Lila confide, and relieve some of her burden by sharing it.

"Lila will tell me what's going on when she's ready, Rev Robbie," admonishes Judith. "She knows I'm a willing listener, I've told her repeatedly, but she needs to come to me in her own time."

"No, I think you're wrong there, Judith," he replies. "How long have you been waiting for Lila to come to you?"

Judith experiences a moment's discomfort when she realizes it has been weeks. "Um, I guess it's been about a month. A bit more than that actually," she admits.

"Well then. It's obvious that Lila has been deeply hurt and she needs some help, a push, to see her way clear."

"Hey confession is your line, not mine, so why don't you coax the truth out of her?"

"Oh I've tried. Unfortunately I don't have the authority of a priest. Lila's Catholic, or I might have been able to browbeat her into telling me."

"That sounds a bit heavy-handed!" laughs Judith seeing the twinkle in the elderly man's eyes.

"I do admit that back in the day I sometimes envied my Catholic counterparts for the rigid control they had over their parishioners."

"I think Lila is what they call a *lapsed Catholic*."

"I'm pretty sure the Catholic Church doesn't even acknowledge such a state! But no, I tried several times and got no where. I think it would do her a world of good to share her secret with you and with God."

"Doesn't God already know?" teases Judith.

"Of course He does! but it's still important that Lila tells Him herself."

Judith retreats from a theological discussion about her friend, it makes her feel she is prying, and their talk returns to accountancy.

* * * * * *

Lila spots Judith's car pulling into The Centre's parking lot just as she reaches the front doors. She doesn't wait for her friend but enters the building on her own. The volleyball players are milling around the foyer, dressed to play and ready to get started, but complaining that the auditorium doors are locked.

The Centre itself is always open during the day and evening, but not the gym unless a game is scheduled. The hardwood floors need plenty of the TLC provided by Mr. Miller and his son, the custodians, to keep them in good shape. Outdoor shoes can only be worn for the walk from the door to the bleachers.

"Kyle's got keys, is he here somewhere?" asks Lila.

"If he is he's hiding—" says one of the players.

"Yeah, and we know why!" interrupts her team-mate. A few sniggers are heard followed by some loud whispering and giggles.

Lila announces she'll go get Rev Robbie who must have lost track of the time. She heads to his office down the hall, her nurses' shoes making no sound.

The team-mates wait until the silence is broken by a cry from Lila. They surge forward in a group, including Judith who has arrived at one end of the hall and Patricia who appears at the other end. With tears streaming down her face Lila waves everyone back and chokes out that someone needs to call 9-1-1 for an ambulance and the police.

"The police!" everyone starts questioning at once except Judith who makes the emergency call and then phones Grant as well. She has no idea he is already at work in the building.

Pat switches into her Principal Johnson role and instructs the young people to go to the change-rooms and get back into their regular clothes. They won't be able to play tonight. They'll have to wait until the police arrive but there is no point getting chilled in their uniforms of shorts and t-shirts.

Judith moves forward purposefully against the tide of teenagers. She joins Pat and Lila in the doorway of Rev Robbie's office to see the man lying on the floor with his frail limbs contorted. They don't go further inside the small, sparsely furnished room. Lila says she'd already checked him for vital signs and found none.

A whitish substance, like foam, dribbles over his lower lip and chin, and his teeth are bared in a grimace. It is the most horrible sight any of the women has ever seen.

"He's had some sort of fit," says Pat in a shocked whisper.

"No, he's been poisoned," replies Lila flatly.

Judith gasps and is about to ask if Lila is sure, but stops herself knowing that of course her friend, the nurse, is certain. She has to strain to hear Lila's anguished muttering:

"What am I going to do now? I was counting on him to help me."

Chapter Four

Saturday, December 28, 2019

"Hey Judith," says Lila answering her cellphone.

"Hi, it's... oh, you know it's me. Okay listen, Grant came by and gave me some tickets, it's the strangest offer, but I said I'd ask you anyhow."

"Oooh, that sounds intriguing! What's it all about?"

"He was *gifted*, he said, dinner for two at that Indian casino on the edge of town – a buffet apparently – but he can't go so he suggested you and I use the tickets. What do you think? would you want to do that?"

"Are you kidding? of course! The food there is really good. I don't know about being gifted, though. Was it a comp? is Grant a player?"

"At the casino? I don't think so. Why would you think that?"

"Well if you're a regular and you spend enough money you get complimentary – comp – stuff."

"Oh, I see what you mean. No, he got the tickets as his gift from the Secret Santa draw they had at their Christmas party at the police station. So, you do want to go?"

"For sure! it will be a blast. I'll drive because I've been there before and getting onto the grounds is a bit tricky because of construction."

"Oh you've been before? Good, because I haven't. What should I wear?"

"Casual clothes, something comfortable. Last time I was at a casino I saw a guy wearing a pyjama top tucked into his jeans. He obviously thought it was a regular shirt and no doubt figured he got a great price on it! You'll see people in work coveralls, hooker gear, wedding parties, you name it.

Casinos are great equalizers. You get people of every colour and creed sitting at a table united against the dealer, or rather *the House*' It's all about playing together to beat the House."

"I don't want to gamble, I just want to have dinner and definitely take the opportunity to look around a little - if they allow that?"

"Sure. You don't have to gamble, and there's no cover charge or anything. It'll be fun, you'll see. Let me just finish up what I'm doing here and I can get you in about 45 minutes, is that okay?"

"Um, yeah sure. What time does the casino open?"

Lila laughs as she answers: "You're better off asking what time does it close? which is only for about five or six hours out of every twenty-four, seven days a week, unless you play poker and that's continuous. We aren't Vegas yet, but we're getting there."

"I can see I'm in for an education going to a casino with you," replies Judith.

"You can be sure of that and, seriously, the food will be fantastic so I hope you're hungry. See you soon."

* * * * * *

Judith has driven by the big new hotel on the outskirts of Calgary but didn't realize it houses a casino. There are a couple of buildings and a huge parking lot that is packed.

Judith is surprised, she didn't realize a night out at the casino would be so popular. She wonders if it is only busy at weekends. Lila has explained that there are five casinos in the city and another Indian casino halfway to Banff.

"What's the difference?"

"Difference between...?"

"All the casinos. You said there's five but then you specifically mention Indian casinos. Are they different?"

"Oh probably, but I couldn't tell you why. It will have something to do with being on reservation land. Maybe the rules are different? I do know that the Province has authority over gambling but the reservation is Federal jurisdiction so that might have something to do with it."

"Are there really enough gamblers in this city to support that many casinos?"

"Oh yeah. Of course some are busier than others – location does matter – and what kind of parking is available, stuff like that. Anyhow, we're here so let's have some fun."

Lila spots a car pulling out and drives over to wait for the space. It is close to the main doors. The unseasonably warm temperatures have turned the lot slushy but neither woman complains. Wearing boots is a small price to pay to avoid the bitterly cold windy weather more common at this time of year.

They enter the warm lobby and, smelling cigarette smoke, Lila says:

"I remember now, one of the differences is that customers can smoke in the Indian casinos."

"I can smell it, remember when everywhere smelled like this?"

"Yeah, I have to confess that I never noticed the smell when I smoked. It's embarrassing to say now but back then I even smoked between courses at meals. And in restaurants, too!"

"You were a smoker? but you're a nurse!"

"Well I wasn't always a nurse, I used to be a kid! I started smoking in Grade Nine so at thirteen or fourteen years old 'cause all the cool kids smoked so naturally... but you'd be surprised how many nurses and doctors do smoke – even nowadays. Those minutes of camaraderie while you're huddled outside to feed your addiction can be a great stress reliever from a demanding job."

"I've never smoked."

"I can't say that surprises me, Judith. Do you want to check your jacket? I don't think I'll bother."

"No, but do you want to eat first and then look around? I'm kinda hungry."

"That's a good idea, otherwise if we get stuck at a blackjack table or on a machine we might end up missing dinner!"

"Lila, that's not going to happen. Believe me."

Lila laughs with her friend and they head towards the restaurant with Judith's head swivelling left to right taking in all the sights. She is surprised at the number of customers there, and notices the varying ages and races.

A slot machine blares triumphant music and she stops to watch the flashing lights and colourful, swirling graphics.

"It's a penny slot and all that hoo-hah is for about $50.00," comments Lila.

"$50.00 is an excellent return for a penny!" exclaims Judith.

"True, but you probably have to bet about 25 pennies per spin to hit bonus payouts, and you can spin three or four times a minute - maybe more - I'll show you later."

"This is the ugliest carpet I've ever seen," comments Judith looking down at the garishly coloured haphazard patterns of the floor covering.

"It's supposed to be. The decor of a casino is very carefully thought-out and planned. They don't want you looking down, you should be looking up at the slot machines, attracted by the bells and whistles and flashing lights. The loudest, and supposedly more frequently paying, machines are at the end of the rows to grab your attention as you walk by. The mirrored walls reflect back the lights and simultaneously make the rooms look larger and more crowded. Gamblers are turned on by the buzz, the noise, and the action.

An Indian casino probably doesn't go in for Feng Shui but some casinos in town have hired professionals to do their cosmic energy thing, it's something to do with harmonizing individuals with their surroundings. Obviously, I don't know much about it but I did spot a golden dragon statue way up high on top of the door-sill at another casino and that would have been put there for good luck."

"Good luck for the players or the House?" asks Judith.

"I guess for whoever believes in it."

There is a fairly long line-up when they arrive at the restaurant but a sign directs Buffet Patrons to go down a short corridor. Judith hands over the tickets to the hostess waiting there and is told to hang on to them until it is time to pay their bill.

The woman adds that the tickets don't include alcoholic beverages but soft drinks, coffee, or tea are no charge. She leads them to a table for four so they have room to pile their coats on a spare chair. As soon as the hostess steps away a server comes forward with a water jug and a menu of drink specials.

"Since I'm driving I can only have one drink so I'll make it a glass of the house red. Why don't you try a mocktail? That's a cocktail with no booze in it."

"I'll pass on that, thanks," answered Judith, "but I will have a ginger-ale, please."

After the server leaves Judith turns to Lila saying:

"It's not very busy, is it?"

"No, but it's still early for the Saturday night crowd. Also, it's very expensive. That long line we sashayed past was for the main restaurant which is menu service and cheaper."

"I don't *sashay*," laughs Judith.

"Well you should!" retorts Lila explaining: "You've certainly got the booty for it."

They don't have much opportunity to look around before their server is back with the drinks and telling them to go up to the buffet whenever they are ready.

"Please take your purses with you, but your coats will be fine where they are."

Judith and Lila stand up with Judith whispering, "Of course I'm taking my purse."

Lila didn't exaggerate when she spoke of a great meal. There is seafood, beef, ham, chicken, Italian dishes, Chinese dishes, Ukrainian food, and even a vegetarian casserole in addition to salads of all kinds, raw veggies with dip, a variety of fresh fruit, potatoes cooked three different ways, two kinds of rice, dumplings, and several vegetables.

"Just take a small bit of each thing and then you can come back for a second serving of whatever you liked best. Remember to leave room for dessert as well."

"I took lots of fruit. It's so expensive to buy at this time of year but look, I got pineapple and strawberries and raspberries."

"There was mango and kiwi fruit too, didn't you see it?"

"I did, but I don't know if I like those fruits."

"Well that's the whole point of buffet – you get to have a taste of new stuff. Judith, you really need to get out more!"

Judith waves off Lila's teasing knowing it is good-natured. Besides, it's true. She does need to spread her wings a little. Imagine if she came here with Grant and made a fool of herself? But no, he wouldn't embarrass her or anything, he is a good friend.

They both eat with enjoyment and take another trip to the hot dishes, but make sure to visit the dessert tables as well. Neither woman can resist heaping a plate from the temptingly presented chocolate-dipped fruit, cakes, pies, squares, cookies, and ice-cream with do-it-yourself topping selections.

"I'm stuffed," announces Lila with a satisfied smile.

"Me too! You're right about the food here, everything is delicious."

"I'll phone Grant to thank him but you'll have to find a better way to show your appreciation of the wonderful feast we just had."

Lila wiggles her eyebrows suggestively and Judith smiles saying:

"Hmmm, I won't ask you for advice in that department."

Lila's face falls as she says: "No, I'm obviously not an expert in relationships these days," with a big sigh.

Judith chastises herself for saying something that reminds her friend of her failing marriage.

"Oh, I didn't mean—"

"I know you didn't, and I'm resolved to having a good time tonight, no moping over Arnie. I did enough of that over my first Christmas without him. So, let's settle the bill and then we'll try our luck on the gaming floor."

They both contribute a good tip to the delight of their waitress who tells them most people don't tip at a buffet since they have to serve themselves.

"But you brought us drinks and cleared away our used plates."

"Several times!" adds Lila. "We did get table service and it was great, thank you."

"Good luck to you both, I really hope you win," says the girl.

* * * * * *

An hour later both women are ready to head home after walking all around the casino. They have looked in the poker room, where the players seemed to hunch over their cards; and in the high-limit room where the amount of the high-value chips being wagered shocks Judith;

and then they checked out all the different table games and money wheels and slots machines.

Lila said she isn't in the mood to sit down at a table and play cards but she would like to try her luck with a few spins at roulette. She leads them over to the table she wants to play.

Lila buys playing chips and places her bets. Soon the layout is full of coloured chips and the little white ball is whizzing round the wheel. As it clatters to a halt everyone, including Judith, leans forward to see where it landed after bouncing twice. The dealer announces the winning number and its colour and, somehow, marks its location despite stacks of playing chips covering all the squares. Judith is fascinated.

The croupier, as Lila explains he's called, is very skilled. He moves smoothly and maintains his smile even while some customers are grumbling at him.

Lila wins on some spins and loses on the others explaining to Judith that although she lost her column bets she won on the inside which pays more so she is up a bit. Judith isn't sure what Lila means, but is happy for her friend.

She changes the roulette chips for money chips and gives the dealer a tip, he thanks her nicely.

Judith notices that almost all of the casino workers are members of *visible minorities* and she wonders if these are government-subsidized positions? Strong English-language skills – particularly written – wouldn't be essential in a job dealing cards. In fact, there is very little conversation going on, mostly the only voices heard are from the dealers counting the hands out loud.

It would be good work experience for newcomers to the country. Many immigrants, as well as Canadians from other provinces, gravitate to Calgary. Its young population, high-paying jobs in the energy sector, and proximity to half-a-dozen provincial and federal parks makes it popular.

Everyone wears a uniform of black pants and long-sleeved, high-necked shirts in solid colours of teal-blue or maroon at the tables, and forest-green at the slot machines. The security guards wear all-black and the supervisors dress in black blazers over white shirts.

Lila shows Judith the chips she's received from the roulette table when she cashed out.

"See these are money chips which I can play at any table, but I'll have to go to the banker's cage to cash them out."

Judith studies the chips with interest but doesn't want to touch them saying they are probably very germy.

"Uh yeah, thanks for that. Now what about you, you've had a look around at the different games so do you want to try something?"

"Yes, I'm going to invest twenty dollars in one of those million-dollar slot machines over there."

"It would be so cool if you won with beginner's luck!"

Heading towards that particular bank of slot machines Judith comes face-to-face with Andrea Seely, a demanding and overbearing school parent she would have avoided if she'd seen her coming.

Both ladies exclaim at the same time: "What are you doing here?"

"I'm part of a bachelorette party, we figured with our social standing visiting a male strip club was out of the question but these casinos give half their profits to charities – by law – so it seemed like a good idea, and fun too."

"Lila and I got free tickets to the dinner buffet and we recommend it. We both ate a wonderful meal with a huge variety of well-prepared foods."

"Lucky you! I heard that the buffet here is a bit on the pricey side but it's because of all the seafood."

"Yes, well I'm hoping I'm also lucky on that slot machine over there."

Andrea Seely's participation in the conversation has been mechanical but now she looks at Judith with interest.

"You like playing the slots, do you?"

"I don't know, I've never tried before. Do you play them?"

"Not really, I'm looking around enjoying the atmosphere. It's real 'slice of life' stuff, isn't it?"

"Where is your party?"

"Scattered about. It turns out a couple of them are Vegas regulars so they're whooping it up at the Craps table and I think a few more are cheering them on. In fact, I'm heading that way myself."

The women move in opposite directions. As they reach the *Million Dollar Jackpot* machine Judith chose she looks at Lila asking:

"She seemed awfully interested in me playing the slot machines – do you think she's worried that I'm gambling away the School's tuition fees?"

"I think she's just a nosy snob."

"Ahhh, so does a million-dollar slot machine fit with my social standing?"

Lila laughingly replies:

"If you win a million bucks you can have whatever standing you like! Just don't spend it all on perfume!"

"Omigod yes! the woman just reeks of scent. Some places, like dental offices, won't even let people wear it any more because of allergies. Especially when it's put on so strongly that it's overpowering like that! By the way, when we're back in the car remind me to tell you a story Pat Johnson passed on about Mrs. Seeley."

"Oooh, juicy gossip?"

"I thought so!"

Judith feeds the money into the bill slot, reads the 'how to play' instructions and chooses a maximum bet for $3 then she pushes the Spin button. She is disappointed at not getting to pull on a handle but Lila explains the 'one-armed bandits' are a thing of the past. The first spin produces nothing but the second spin pays out seventy dollars which Judith promptly cashes out.

"You don't want to play anymore?"

"No, of course not. I've got my original twenty back *and* I'm up fifty bucks!"

"But I thought you were going to spend twenty to invest on a million-dollar chance?"

"Oh Lila, it's that kind of thinking that got the jackpot up to a million in the first place."

Chapter Five

After dropping Judith off in the half-circle drive of her apartment building Lila waits to see her friend safely unlock the front door. Instead, Judith turns suddenly and hurries back to the car saying:

"I just remembered, I was going to share some hot gossip about Andrea Seely."

"That's right! get in again, it's too chilly to stand outside."

Lila puts the car in park while Judith climbs back in the front-seat, pausing to recollect exactly the conversation she'd recently had with Pat which she then passes on.

"Pat started with this long speech saying since I've never been chummy with my coworkers I'm not part of the gossip grapevine. She knows I hear things in passing, but usually don't know any details so I don't have a bias or false information. *Fake news,* as they call it nowadays.

It wouldn't be appropriate for Pat, as School Principal, to hang out in the staffroom sharing tidbits but she said I'm always discreet. But what makes me so valuable to her as a listener is that I'm a fresh audience. Also she complimented me by saying I have good insights into *why* so-and-so *did* do such-and-such, and I'm always willing to speculate as to motive. From all of that flattery I figure her husband, Mark, isn't the least bit interested in discussing this stuff. So, anyways, that's the background. Here's what she said:

Judith replayed the entire scene in her mind and relayed it from memory.

"Mark and I belong to the Horticultural Society, as I think I've mentioned before," said Pat and Judith nodded, not commenting that Pat had actually mentioned it many, many times before. "And we've been at The Centre quite a bit lately because during the winter we have the time to listen to speakers and presentations, work on Society bylaws, memberships, newsletters – things we're too busy to deal with once the gardening year is in full swing."

"I've heard from more than one person that no matter how nice the Spring weather might be there's no point planting until after the May long weekend, is that when your season starts?"

"Pretty much. I mean, what you heard is true but goodness knows how often we've forgotten and been misled by false Spring into hurrying into the season before the snow has finished with us!" laughed Pat. "It's also the first big camping weekend of the year and it invariably turns cold, rainy and – very often – snowy!"

"Ugh, I have absolutely no interest in camping and, since I live in an apartment building, no need to garden."

"Oh! but there's quite a bit you could do with indoor plants, and you have a balcony, and what about east-facing windows? my plants just thrive in that location."

"Hmm, maybe I could go with you on one of your trips to the garden centre and you can advise me on some selections. Every now and then I pick up something at the grocery store but they never last."

"Oh, you don't want to buy from there! Those plants are no good," exclaimed Pat.

"Well, I still have a poinsettia I got from Costco a few Christmases ago."

"Yes, well Costco is different. I'd be delighted to take you, and actually there's a new plant nursery I'm looking forward to visiting so we'll go there. Although I have to admit I can get a bit carried away, Judith, so we each better take our own vehicle or you'll end up stuck there much longer than you'd like!" Pat laughed again. She has such a deep chuckle that it's impossible to resist joining in.

"Okay, it's a date," declared Judith. "But that's not why you came to visit me at my desk so what's on your mind?"

"Oh, I just had to talk to someone about that Andrea Seely. You'll never believe what she's been up to... and that poor young man, he doesn't know which way to turn. She's always there in hot pursuit and she must have twenty years on him – at least!"

"What young man and what won't I believe? Frankly, I think I can believe anything about Andrea Seely. I really dislike that woman. Oh I know I shouldn't say that about a parent but honestly..."

"Well she's out-done herself this time. She's set her sights on Kyle Danby, the Sports Director?"

"The name doesn't ring a bell, I don't know him."

"Oh, he's a lovely young man, so polite and friendly, smart, very diplomatic, he'll definitely get on in life. And he's such a handsome guy as well, mixed blood often produces outstanding features. His mother is Asian, from Indonesia I think? and his father is Black. I know Kenneth Danby from our Church but not Mrs. Danby, she doesn't attend. I believe she's Muslim but non-practising or something.

Anyhow, I've known Kyle since he was just a little fellow and now he's in his early twenties and extremely tall. You know he wanted to be a pilot but there's a height restriction and he outgrew the limits. Isn't that interesting? normally when there are height issues it's because someone isn't tall enough but apparently, with the air force, there's a standard size to cockpits so they have a maximum height."

"Oh that is interesting, that would never have crossed my mind. But we're getting sidetracked. What does Andrea Seely have to do with Kyle... Danby, you said?"

"Yes, Kyle Danby. Well she's making such an obvious play for him that it's embarrassing for everyone around them! He tries to avoid her but she's shameless, doesn't care who she involves in her attempts to form an intrigue or whatever with this poor guy. She's constantly poking her nose into one room after the next asking 'is Kyle in here?' or 'I'm trying to find Kyle, have you seen him?' She's making a laughingstock out of herself."

"Oh, ewww," Lila interrupts, screwing up her face in disgust.

"I know, eh?" I said to her: "Oh, don't make me feel sorry for Andrea Seely, I quite *like* disliking her."

"Ha-ha, I know what you mean. Sorry for butting in, go on with what Pat said."

"She said: Yes, she does have that effect on people, doesn't she? Awful woman."

"Isn't this Kyle very young to be a Sports Director?"

"Well it's a case of big title in lieu of decent pay. He probably doesn't get much more than minimum wage but he's taking classes at the University so this is a part-time job for him. He's a godsend during the summer, though. The Centre is busy year-round, particularly on weekends, but summertime it's full all week with day-camp programmes for the school-age children on vacation. Some of our teachers volunteer their time which I think is so good of them."

"It is, we've got some great people on staff."

"And then there's Marta..." Pat stage-whispered.

"I'll bet she can tell you all the ins and outs of the Andrea Seely/Kyle Danby affair, or wanna-be affair, plus plenty of salacious details true or otherwise."

"Oh no doubt she could but listening to her would make me feel dirty."

"Pat really said that?!" exclaims Lila with delight.

"Yes, and when she did I was the one who gave a loud laugh!"

"That Pat is so funny, eh? But jeez, Andrea Seely is a married woman and a mother. What the heck is she doing chasing around after some young guy? and so publicly, too!"

"Well Lila, even I've heard of *cougars*. Andrea's not old and she's well... a bit chunky but you could call that voluptuous..."

"Only if you're very kind – or blind!"

"Stop, she's not that bad."

"Judith she's certainly not a MILF! oh I feel for that poor fellow being pursued by an overpowering harpy like her!"

"Do I want to know what a MILF is?"

"Ask Grant," Lila replies with a devilish smile.

Chapter Six

Lila and Judith plan to bring in the new year together. They choose to celebrate at Lila's place so she can have a drink, and Judith can drive home sober as ever. Lila enjoys cooking and has promised a feast of tasty nibbles, sweet treats, and fattening junk food.

Judith has seen Grant a few times over the holiday week, with and without Lila in attendance, but he hasn't mentioned doing anything on New Year's Eve. It's likely he has to work. and Judith doesn't mind because she wants to spend some one-on-one time with Lila.

Her friend has put a good face on things at Christmas and the days following, but Judith can see she is sad. Lila has had a couple of outings with Beth Penner and her father Brian, a combined trip of lunch and shopping the Boxing Day sales, and a day out ice-skating.

Judith knows Lila finds the widower very attractive – well he is a handsome, well-built man. Has she told him she's married? It's the state of that marriage that is causing Lila her unhappiness. Judith is pretty sure the marriage is over.

"What time do you want me tonight? and can I bring anything?" Judith asks when she calls Lila in the afternoon.

"Come whenever you like, the only schedule we have is midnight countdown and singing 'Auld Lang Syne'. Oh you could bring a bottle of champagne, I thought I had one but I don't."

"Oh! I could, I guess... is there a liquor store on the way to you? I've never been to one. Do they take credit cards? I do have some cash on me... what kind should I buy?"

"Ha-ha," laughed Lila, "I got you good. I'm just joking, I've got two bottles of champagne chilling in case you change your mind about joining me. You can always crash on the couch. You really don't have a clue about booze, do you?"

"You did have me going! And I'll have you know I know plenty about booze just not from personally indulging – thank God. I might as well explain because you won't let up, will you?

My mother was an alcoholic who drank herself to death. There was only me to deal with her so my hands-on experience was cleaning up stinking messes and listening to a constant litany of self-pity and recriminations from when I was in primary school. As a result, to this day, I can't stand the smell of wine, beer, or liquor."

"Oh Judith, I am so sorry. I promise to never pester you about it again." Lila does sound contrite and Judith, surprised that the admission had been relatively painless says:

"You know it's probably a good thing for me to get it out in the open. You see no one ever knew, it was Mum's secret, but it became mine as well. I guess I could have told someone – a teacher, or neighbour – but somehow I knew it wasn't something to share, it was something to hide."

"Oh you poor thing. You were forced to grow up when you should have been a carefree kid."

"I don't think I'd ever have been that carefree..."

"No, maybe not," agrees Lila. "Anyhow, come over when you like, I'm just wearing a fleece track suit, and just come as you are because I've got everything we need."

Judith has already bought a box of Lila's favourite treats: *Hedgehogs* from Purdy's Chocolates, so she certainly won't be arriving empty-handed.

* * * * * *

The two women enjoy their feast of snack foods while watching some TV but mostly talking. They talk and talk about themselves, their work, their relationships.

Although Judith has had a wonderful night she detects the underlying sadness when Lila talks about herself. It looks like her marriage, after all these years, has now failed and that's weighing her down. She was so disappointed that Arnie still refused to open up to her despite saying he wanted their marriage to continue. And, of course, not coming to see her for Christmas.

Once Lila has talked her feelings out Judith lets the subject drop. She doesn't feel qualified to give relationship advice, and having never met Arnie she can't even take on the role of knowledgeable bystander.

They count down the New Year and toast it with a glass of champagne clinking against a glass of ginger-ale. Lila points out that Judith's glass has more bubbles than hers does.

"Serves me right for choosing the stuff that was on sale but I'm actually not a big fan of champagne so I figured it wouldn't really matter."

"You've heard the advice that *you should always buy the best you can afford?* well the corollary to that is *and you should also be satisfied with it.* So you might as well enjoy what's you've got."

It's cold and frosty at two in the morning when Judith drives home. It's easy to find your way around Edgemont Village with numbered streets, few traffic lights, and no one-ways. The planners deliberately made the roads curvy to keep traffic moving at slower speeds, but the many bends and turns can be challenging in winter weather.

Judith is alert to her surroundings and keeps an eye on the few cars she sees, being especially careful at intersections in case some drunk driver is going to barrel through against the light.

She sees a red row of tail-lights ahead and figures it's a CheckStop by the police looking for impaired drivers, but once she gets closer she realizes the cars have stopped to let a few dogs ... no, they are coyotes ... cross the road. She watches the animals bound into the wooded area on the far side of the road and wonders for a moment if it's coyotes or wolves that have such bushy tails.

Seeing the animals trotting along so unconcerned, so confident, so carefree, seems like a good omen for the new year.

Chapter Seven

Wednesday, January 1, 2020

On Wednesday, the first day of the *twenties*, Judith wakes up to a text from Grant wishing her all the best for the new year. She texts back good wishes and, smiling at her own daring, adds that the school is closed until the following Monday. He replies that he is off Friday night and would she like to get together for a meal?

JUDITH: sounds gr8 thx

GRANT: + movie 2

JUDITH: whats on

GRANT: no clue what do u like

JUDITH: comedy, mystery

GRANT: terminator sequel #1 doctor sleep #2

JUDITH: scary s king novel what else

GRANT: ford v ferrari

JUDITH: whos in it

GRANT: matt damon

JUDITH: sounds ok

GRANT: fri matinee dinner

JUDITH: perfect

GRANT: tty fri am

JUDITH: k bye

Judith spends the rest of her day doing laundry, taking down the few Christmas decorations she'd put up, and cleaning the apartment. She likes to have the place fresh and tidy for the new year.

Then she tackles a personal tidy-up with a manicure, pedicure, leg shaving, and eyebrow tweezering. Having accomplished a lot on this, the first day of the new year, she relaxes with a long soak in a bubble-bath before donning her flannelette pyjamas.

Scrubbed pink and feeling warm and cozy she settles on the couch with hot chocolate and her laptop to watch a show on Netflix. Grant has recommended a TV series that started a few years ago called "The Blacklist" and so far she is really enjoying it.

* * * * * *

"Who is calling me so early in the morning!" complains Judith when her cellphone rings loudly. Each night she plugs it into the charger in the outlet behind the dresser, the phone propped up to serve as her clock. Squinting she can see that it reads 09:09 – angel numbers – and it's really not early at all.

I probably shouldn't have stayed up watching those last two episodes," she thinks, *"but they end on such cliffhangers! I couldn't resist."*

The caller ID shows that it is Lila calling so Judith tries to sound bright and awake when she answers.

"Oh no, I woke you up!"

"No, well yes but I should be up anyhow. It's after nine."

"Good well, I'm bursting and had to tell someone. Arnie phoned, and he's coming to see me! He's off until Monday as well so he's flying in, he'll arrive this evening, and we'll finally get to sit down face-to-face and hash things out. I am so relieved. I have to admit that Christmas was really hard without him."

"Oh I'm really happy for you, Lila. When did he call?"

"Just now. Well, I guess it was actually about an hour ago, he's two hours ahead of us. We talked a lot, I mean we both miss each other so much, and well... I'm so happy. I can't wait to see him!"

"I hope I get a chance to meet him too although I don't want to intrude, you only have a few days together."

"You're definitely going to meet him. How about you and Grant double-dating with us? We can go out for a nice steak dinner at The Keg on Saturday, oh wait it will be packed and they don't take reservations. We'll figure out a place."

"Maybe Arnie would like to see Banff?"

"That's a terrific idea! There's a Keg there, or Tony Roma's, or wow there are quite a few places to eat so we'll find something for sure."

"I'll ask Grant but I'm actually seeing him on Friday night for a movie–"

"So you see him two nights in a row, that's okay."

"Well, I'll ask him but I want you to clear it with Arnie first, he might just want you all to himself."

"Judith you do know how many years we've been married, right?"

"Yeah so? You haven't seen each other for months."

"Oh, I'd better let Mrs. Piernitsky know that he's coming tonight and who he is. She'll probably cook something. I'll do that right now before

I forget. Then I've got to go get some groceries, stop at the liquor store, clean up the place.. Okay bye, Judith!"

She disconnects before Judith realizes her *good luck* comment has gone unheard. Judith can picture Lila bouncing from room to room tidying, checking cupboards and fridge to make a shopping list in her head, a whirlwind of blonde curls as she prepares for the husband she hasn't seen in months.

Judith finds she is smiling at the good news although she realizes it will probably mean that Lila will move back to Toronto. It isn't a happy thought to lose her friend, but she does have Grant in her life now.

Chapter Eight

Friday, January 3, 2020

Judith isn't sure what to do. She doesn't want to intrude on Lila and Arnie's time together but she hasn't heard anything since Thursday's phone call. Until this morning's text arrived.

A text from Lila usually involved lots of exclamation points or question marks, uppercase words, and emojis of hearts and smileys, frownies, or WTF graphics. Today's text was simple:

LILA: cancel sat dinner sorry ttyl

Judith had immediately replied:

JUDITH: no prob is ev ok

That was hours ago and she hasn't heard a thing. So she'd phoned but her call went to voicemail. She hung up and tried again but same result. Unsure what to say in a message Judith chose to say nothing. Lila would see from the call history who had phoned. Now Judith was undecided, wondering if she should call again.

Instead, she chose to finish getting ready since Grant would be arriving soon to take her to the afternoon show.

Judith has deliberately dressed down to go to the theatre. She puts on older clothes that she will immediately toss in the wash when she gets back home. Sometimes she'd see moviegoers wearing shorts and she'll shudder to think of their bare legs rubbing against the seats. She always wears socks and running shoes as well, nothing is going to crawl up her leg!

Looking in the mirror she acknowledges to herself that even in this old sweatshirt Lila's comments about her figure being shapely are accurate.

She wants to look nice for Grant, he has good dress-sense and always looks just right for the occasion, but the movie theatre is well... not clean by Judith's standards.

She decides she won't say anything about Lila and tomorrow's cancellation until after the show when they stop for a bite to eat.

Judith had called Grant after talking to Lila to mention the Saturday night dinner invitation. When he said Sure, that sounds interesting she'd given him an out for Friday but he'd insisted on keeping their Friday date as well.

Judith toys with the idea that maybe things are becoming serious, but realizes it's only the rare circumstance of Lila's estranged husband's visit that means having two dates in two days.

* * * * * *

Grant spends more money at the concession stand than he's paid for their tickets to the show. But the snacks are filling because after a large popcorn, large drink, and a chocolate bar each neither feels like dinner.

Judith is annoyed that she's worn a dark sweatshirt since it shows up every tiny bit of popcorn that she's managed to spill over herself.

"How about coffee and a doughnut at Tim Horton's? My treat," she suggests.

"Actually, I'm in the mood for ice-cream."

"It's still winter!"

"Dairy Queen is open, do you like soft-serve?"

"I love Dairy Queen. My favourite is a chocolate-dipped cone but I usually get a sundae because when it's hot outside the cones melt and drip so fast."

"Well, it's not hot now so you can have your first choice. I like butterscotch sundaes so long as it's butterscotch and not caramel."

"Chocolate is my favourite flavour, but caramel is okay. I don't care for butterscotch. Lots of people can't tell the difference. You really prefer butterscotch?"

"Definitely, I have a refined palate."

Judith laughs answering: "Well you can't prove it by what you've eaten today."

Grant has to agree. He drives them to a Dairy Queen restaurant and she's surprised to see several people inside, after all it is January. She mentions this to Grant who tells her that the burgers are pretty good as well as the ice cream.

He asks the server if the sundaes are butterscotch or caramel and she gives him a confused look before saying they're the same flavour. When he says no, they aren't, she goes to ask someone in the kitchen area.

"If she has to ask," he explains to Judith, "That means it's not butterscotch."

Sure enough when the girl returns she says they have caramel, adding it's practically the same thing. Grant doesn't want to argue so he orders two large chocolate-dipped cones instead then steps aside to let Judith pay.

"Thank you," she says once they choose a table and sit down with their desserts.

"Why thank me? you paid!"

"And you let me do so without an argument. Also, I'm glad you didn't argue with the girl about butterscotch versus caramel."

"Well she's a teenager so nothing I say would penetrate anyhow."

"Teenagers aren't stupid, they're just young."

"No, I didn't say stupid, I just mean that there's nothing I can ever say that will be more important to her than the thoughts currently occupying her mind. Her clothes, her make-up, her girlfriends, her boyfriends, her plans for the weekend... all those things are swirling around in her head. I'm just a brief interruption who is then quickly forgotten. Believe me I am infinitely patient with young people, I have five nephews and four nieces."

"Oh my! big family."

"It is now. There were just the three of us growing up but both of my sisters love being Moms."

"Christmas must be a blast!"

Grant thinks he hears a faintly wistful tone in Judith's voice. He answersbriskly:

"Christmas is damn expensive!" and they both laugh.

"On a more serious topic I have to let you know tomorrow's dinner is cancelled, and I need your advice."

"What's up?"

Judith explains about Lila's uncharacteristically brief text message and subsequent lack of response to text and phone calls.

"I don't know if I should leave a message. I don't want to interrupt them but all of this is so unlike Lila that I'm a bit concerned. What do you think?"

Grant considers for a few moments before saying:

"I'm not sure, Judith. I mean I don't know her well and I don't know him at all. I really can't say."

"Well, what would do if you were me?"

"Hmm. I guess leaving a message wouldn't hurt but personally I wouldn't bother. She knows you've called and they're either in the middle of a massive fight or well... the opposite. Either way, they're busy."

"Or maybe they finished the fight and now they're enjoying *the opposite*," says Judith with a smile.

"Make-up sex, yes, lucky them!" Grant smiles as well, admiring the way Judith's surprisingly shabby top hints at her curves, but she gives all her attention to her cone. Watching her lick the ice cream drips Grant is momentarily distracted.

"There's no reason why you and I can't have dinner just ourselves tomorrow night, is there?"

"We've both got to eat so sure, let's eat together."

Grant gives her a sharp look but Judith's artless expression leaves him wondering.

Chapter Nine

Saturday, January 4, 2020

Grant pours the last of the red wine from the carafe into his glass. Judith has graciously offered to be the designated driver so he can enjoy some drinks with his meal.

As a treat, Grant has brought her to The Black Angus, Edgemont's oldest and fanciest steakhouse. Built from riverstone the decor is subdued lighting over wood panelling, and snowy linen cloths on tables with plenty of elbow-room.

The menu offers hearty servings of red meat: tomahawks, t-bones, rib steaks, filet mignon, with Alaskan King Crab legs as its surf and turf option. Both Judith and Grant dine well on expertly prepared steaks cooked rare.

The restaurant caters to an older, monied crowd but the bar is a popular weekend drinking spot for singles.

Judith enjoys the opportunity to get all dolled up. Last December Lila had loaned her a dress for Noel Larkin's birthday/Christmas party and afterwards insisted Judith keep it saying:

"It looks so much better on you! You fill it out properly, and have the long legs to set that skirt swirling."

When Judith protests Lila tells her to consider it a re-gifted Christmas present. Grant wasn't invited to that party so he is seeing Judith in the dress for the first time, and is generous with his compliments.

"This is the second Saturday in a row I've eaten an excellent and expensive restaurant meal, thanks to you. And thank you again, Grant, for the casino buffet tickets. Lila and I had a great time.

Did I tell you we ran into Andrea Seely there? she's Margaret's mother and such a pushy, bossy woman."

"So Margaret *comes by it honestly* as they say..."

"That's true! It seems whenever I'm out I always run into somebody associated with the school: a parent, teachers, student–"

"Have you spotted someone here?"

"Yes, a couple of teachers and you know, it looks like they've just gotten engaged! So nice, we've all been waiting for news of this sort. Lila will be pleased for them."

"Where are they?"

"Cozied up nicely over at that banquette, Eddie and Tanya."

"Do you want to go have a word?"

"Oh no, I'd rather let them enjoy their moment. Speaking of enjoying... when I eat in fancy restaurants I usually order two or three appetizers instead of an entree," Judith explains: "That way I get to indulge in a good variety of gourmet cooking. Tonight, though, I felt a craving for red meat and this has been absolutely wonderful. I'm stuffed!"

"It's even tastier when accompanied by this wine–" the rest of Grant's sentence is cut-off by a loud blast of music from the bar. They've both noticed that the crowd gathering there is growing noisier and with the music playing they have to shout to be heard.

Glancing in that direction again Judith notices lots of people laughing with some trying to dance despite the crush.

"Why don't we finish up here then go back to my place for coffee?"

"Good idea! I remember that you serve great coffee," says Grant, agreeing with her suggestion.

"It is good stuff, the brand is called *Kicking Horse*," Judith replies.

"I've heard of that I think," Grant tilts his head while chasing a memory.

"The name comes from the Kicking Horse Pass but the company is actually in Invermere."

"That's it! I've driven through there on the way to Fairmont Hot Springs and must have seen signs or something."

"I haven't been there but a couple of the teachers went in the Fall and had a great time."

"It's a beautiful spot and there's lots to do, lots of different outdoor activities. Definitely worth seeing."

"Good to know. Well, that's the story behind the coffee. I can't stand bitter coffee so I tried a few of their styles and finally settled on *Hola* because I prefer a lighter, milder blend. They have some medium and dark roasts with cute names like *Smart Ass* and *Half Ass* and *Grizzly Claw*."

"I drink all kinds in my job from convenience store to k-cups to the station house sludge... I can't stand an aftertaste."

"I agree, and that's why I like using a French Press."

A popular song comes on and the bar crowd starts clapping and singing along. It is after 10:00 on a Saturday night. Grant settles the bill while Judith wraps a wool scarf around her throat and puts on her coat. She knows they'll feel the cold once they step out of the warm restaurant.

* * * * * *

Sipping coffee, while sitting side-by-side on the couch in Judith's living-room, Grant looks around and says:

"This place does need a cat. I remembered you saying you were thinking of a cat and I thought about getting one for you, you know. But that very day I read a guest column in the newspaper by someone from the Alberta SPCA saying how pets should never be given as surprise Christmas gifts. Or any kind of present if it's a surprise. They said the recipient should always be the one to choose which makes sense. Growing up we always had pets in the house and the animals responded differently to each of us."

"I've never had a pet but I think a cat would be ideal for an apartment. Although a dog would be good for taking on walks."

"True except dog-walking isn't an option it's a twice-daily chore no matter what the weather is like. Even when it's -30 below they still have to go out. And unless you've got a Newfoundlander or some other big hairy creature your dog might hate being out in the bitter cold too! Cats take care of their business indoors."

"Oh, I never thought of that aspect. Does it smell bad?"

"No, not if you keep the litter box clean. And you know you can talk a cat on a walk, just make sure you have a good harness so he or she doesn't escape. We have a leash by-law for pets and that includes cats. It's a good thing because they're too vulnerable to cars and kids and other animals."

"And they kill a lot of birds, too."

"Birds, squirrels, mice... cats are predators. The leash by-law also means we can have a *No-Kill policy* because if the cats aren't out roaming all night they're not dropping litters three or four times a year."

"Hmm, I can see I'm going to have to do a bit of research before I commit to a pet."

"Well they say the Internet was created to share cute cat videos so you'll find plenty of stuff to choose from."

"I guess I better be careful not to put 'pussy videos' in the search engine," she quips and Grant laughs out loud in surprise.

They finish their coffee and putting the mugs back on the table relax back comfortably. Grant slips an arm over Judith's shoulder and says:

"Judith, can I ask why you don't drink?"

"Now you sound like Lila!" she replies.

"Well, it's not totally unheard-of but it's not all that common. The usual reasons for someone being a non-drinker are it's a religious stipulation, or concerns about a family history of alcoholism, or sometimes it's because of a bad experience with alcohol, or the person is on medication."

"In my case it's none of the above. I did talk about this a few weeks ago with Lila and having said it out loud once now it feels easier to say it again:

I don't drink because my mother was a drunk and just the smell of alcohol repulses me. I'm not worried about inheriting alcoholic tendencies because I know I'll never touch the stuff. In fact, I'm not even sure I believe in alcoholism being a disease. Anyhow, drinking just involves too many messy, smelly memories, ugh."

"Oh that's too bad. I'm not going to say *you don't know what you're missing* because you sound pretty definite and I would never try to persuade someone to drink."

"Thanks for that but it doesn't matter, I couldn't possibly be persuaded. The thing is I began helping my mom cover up her problem at a very young age. My father died when I was just starting school and that was devastating to both Mom and me. Anyhow, so far as I recall Mom held it together for about a year or so and then she started bringing a bottle or two when she came home from work, along with her married boss.

I have no brothers or sisters so there was no one to turn to and no help dealing with my grief. Instead I had to take care of my mother, and to keep our home life a secret. And that's how things were until she died."

"Poor thing. I can imagine you as a little girl struggling and worrying."

"Yes, I did worry all the time. Looking back I don't know what I was so worried about, I mean in retrospect if someone had found out about my mother's problem it would probably have been good for me. But maybe not and there's no pointing thinking *what if?* is there?"

"Poor little Judith, or were you a Judy back then?"

"My father called me Judy. I wouldn't let anyone else."

"Not even your Mom?"

"Huh, she called me *Jude* because she could only manage to slur the first syllable. I wouldn't answer to Judy and insisted on being called Judith because I thought it sounded more grown-up."

She rests her head against Grant's chest and his arm tightens around her shoulders. They sit like that in companionable silence for an enjoyable interval before he finally says he'd better get going. Judith walks him to the door saying thank you for the delicious meal. Grant kisses her goodnight and they both pause waiting for the other to deepen that kiss but instead each pulls back with a smile.

Judith goes to bed shortly afterwards and falls asleep quickly and deeply.

Chapter Ten

Monday, January 6, 2020

Judith's first task when she finally gets to her office on January 6th is to create a text graphic for her screensaver. She's chosen a quote from George Bernard Shaw that resonates with her, and she decides it will be her new year's inspiration:

"The possibilities are numerous once we decide to act and not react"

Judith has already put this into practice while walking through the halls of the school by greeting people instead of just replying to their remarks. Everyone notices her new cheerful attitude and responds with smiles except Marta Smith. She completely snubs Judith.

Last year Judith would have loudly sniped back with a comment like *Marta must be getting old since her hearing's going!* but this year she just shrugs her shoulders. She is spotted by a couple of schoolgirls who giggle and Judith knows the story of the encounter will soon spread.

She has visited with Pat Johnson, the principal, chatted with Samira, the school secretary, drunk a coffee in the staff-room, created her motivational screensaver, and is now ready to tackle setting up the books for the new fiscal year.

Judith loves the look of a brand-new, pale-green ledger sheet. She uses an accounting programme as a back-up to her handwritten entries. That wouldn't have been allowed at the major accounting firm where she'd once worked but here Judith is the boss. She settles into her work and is surprised when Cindy Callahan, the part-time librarian who shares Judith's office space, comes in for her afternoon shift.

"Is that the time already?" exclaims Judith. "I've missed lunch and now that I'm thinking about it, I'm starving!"

"Don't you usually have lunch with Lila Morelli?" asks Cindy.

"Yes, you're right. I wonder why she didn't call? Must be busy, like I was, so I'll pop down to her office to see if she wants to head out for a bite." Judith gathers up her purse but before heading out the door she pauses to remark:

"I like your haircut, Cindy. That style really suits you."

The younger woman stares after Judith with her mouth fallen open in surprise.

* * * * * *

Frustrated by no phone calls from Lila over the weekend Judith is anxious to get together with her friend to find out about Arnie's visit. She'd been expecting Lila to drop into the library office sometime during the morning, but now it's already the afternoon and no Lila.

Judith marches down to the Nurse's office ready for a long overdue gossip. When she arrives it's to discover Lila pushing aside a half-eaten sandwich.

"Oh, hi Judith. What can I do for you?" she asks, blatantly disinterested.

Judith is taken aback and stumbles over her reply:

"I wanted us to go have lunch," she says.

"I've already eaten," Lila gestures to her sparse meal. She wraps the remains of the sandwich adding: "Turns out I wasn't hungry anyhow."

Judith stands there nonplussed while Lila sits silently. Finally Judith bursts out with:

"What happened with Arnie?"

"He's gone home. We talked a lot and now I have plenty to think over. When I make some decisions, and am ready to talk about it, I'll let you know."

Lila isn't forthcoming and Judith is left wondering if she's done something wrong. Her home-life growing up had precluded friendships and Judith's relationship with Lila is still very new. New, but very important to her.

She senses Lila is hurting beneath the cold exterior but obviously doesn't want to share. Judith is completely at a loss and doesn't know how to react.

Deciding that she has no choice but to accept Lila's dismissal she leaves the office and heads out of the school to get a quick lunch. She takes comfort thinking of Grant's New Year's card in her purse.

* * * * * *

Judith is watching another episode of 'The Black List' when her phone rings indicating Grant is calling.

"Hi Judith, how was your first day back after the holidays?" he asks.

"Work was great – I love getting set up for a new year – but on a personal level not so great: Lila skipped our lunch date and when I saw her she snubbed me!"

"Why? I thought she was going to catch you up on the news about her husband's visit. You were looking forward to the two of you getting together."

"That's what I thought too! but it's not what happened. Remember how she's been avoiding my calls and wethought she and Arnie must be busy figuring things out between them? well, now I'm wondering if it's something more than that."

"Like what?"

"Like... well, I don't know."

"What exactly did she say to you?"

"Very little, actually. I asked what happened with them and she said they talked a lot and she had to think things over and she'd tell me about it when she was ready."

"Oh."

"What does *oh* mean?"

"Well, it sounds like things aren't good between them, but hey, I really don't like speculating."

"No, I need you to speculate. You know more about this kind of thing than I do."

"Yeah, but I don't want to say the wrong thing and... look, maybe I shouldn't get involved. Lila's asked you to give her some time and I think you should respect that."

"I see. Well you're right, you shouldn't get involved. Oh look at the time I've got to go now."

"Judith, wait—"

"Bye. Grant." She disconnects the call and when he rings again she lets it go to voicemail. Tossing the phone aside she returns to her TV show but finds her concentration has broken. A few moments later her phone dings to signal an incoming text message. Judith reads:

GRANT: dont be mad pls

She realizes she *is* mad at Grant and doesn't care whether or not she is being unreasonable about it. She switches her phone off and goes to bed early.

Chapter Eleven

Tuesday, January 7, 2020

Sometime overnight, while tossing and turning in her bed, Judith decides she has to confront Lila. For Lila's sake and for Grant's. It isn't fair to vent her frustrations on him.

Tuesday morning she is waiting in the school parking lot early, waiting for Lila to arrive. Her car is easy to spot, a white 2-seater convertible that Lila says is a Miata but Grant calls it an MX-5. Judith couldn't care less, she has absolutely no interest in cars other than as a convenience.

Spotting the sportscar as it wheels in Judith hurries over and knocks on the passenger door. Lila reluctantly opens it and Judith climbs in.

"Lila, something is going on and I want to know what it is."

"I told you I'd tell you when I'm ready," snaps Lila.

"Why are you being so... so hostile?" asks Judith. "Our friendship means a lot to me and I thought it did to you as well."

For a moment so brief Judith has to wonder if she's imagined it, Lila's face softens but then her eyes narrow to a glare and she answers:

"Of course it matters but right now you need to back off. I've asked for some space and you need to give it to me."

"That's what Grant says," complains Judith, "But it's obvious that something's wrong. If I'm truly your friend you should turn to me for help and I should be able to give it, or at least give comfort, and be a sounding board or something."

Again, Lila seems to waver but then she says in a sharp, dismissive tone:

"I can't be plainer, Judith. For now just back off."

Lila gets out of her car and without looking back strides toward the school. Judith, forlorn, has no choice but to follow.

Once she gets into her own office Judith turns on her computer and studies the message that's popped up on her screen:

"The possibilities are numerous once we decide to act and not react"

She thinks about that message and decides this can't be about her and her own hurt feelings. Instead, as a good friend, she has to give Lila the distance she wants. Lila knows she will be here for her when needed.

Besides, the two of them have some matching interests and duties that will keep them in contact, for instance they each hold volunteer positions at The Centre. Although Lila is the newcomer to Edgemont Village she is the one who brought Judith in to meet the Rev Robbie with the idea of taking over some, or all, of the bookkeeping in the first place.

Lila is a friendly, outgoing joiner-type and Judith hates to see her friend in this state but she will go along with Lila's request for now. Grant doesn't seem keen to give advice and he is probably wise not to do so. Judith will figure it out on her own.

* * * * * *

Judith has already gotten into bed but finds she can't sleep so she texts Grant:

im sorry i overreacted

and he answers right away:

its ok good to hear from u call me

When he answers the phone Judith begins in a rush, trying to get all her thoughts out at once:

"I'm not going to talk for long because I'm already in bed. But I had to apologise. I tried sleeping but my conscience kept me awake, and I had enough tossing and turning last night. I don't like it when we're on the outs and I sure don't want to go through another sleepless night again. Anyhow, I was wrong, and I am really sorry about yesterday."

"Honey, it's okay. Now that you've called everything is good. I didn't get much sleep either."

Judith absorbs the 'honey', spoken so casually, with pleasure.

"Well I won't keep you. I just felt badly because I'd been unfair to you."

"No, it's not all on you, I'm guilty, too because you asked my opinion and I sidestepped," he pauses a moment before asking: "Do you still want to know what I think?"

"Yes, of course I do."

"Okay here goes: I think Arnie told Lila something bad... serious... you know – like maybe he'd had an affair – and she has to decide whether or not she can get past whatever it is to keep the marriage going. And I'm only guessing at infidelity, but whatever it is she needs time and space to think it through. I'm sure once she does she'll tell you all about it.

Lila has a strong personality. She doesn't really seem to be the type who asks everybody else what she should do so, as she said, she'll let you know when she's made up her mind."

Judith is quiet for so long that Grant wonders if he's offended her or something. He's about to speak when she says:

"I understand what you're saying and yes, that does sound like the kind of thing Lila would do but... if I'm really her friend shouldn't she confide in me? I mean, I'm not *everybody* I'm... well, I guess I'm not – or rather we're – not the friends I thought we were."

She sounds so sad and forlorn that Grant is wishing he's waited until they are face-to face before voicing his thoughts. It isn't possible to give a hug of comfort in a phone conversation. He doesn't like feeling inadequate.

"Or it could be that Lila is embarrassed or ashamed about whatever it is. She might be *licking her wounds,* so to speak, before sharing the news. It might have been a real shock that's left her not knowing how to react."

"Maybe... I guess I really do just have to be patient and wait."

"Now I want to know the answer too. You'll have to keep my in the loop and in the meantime we'll be curious together."

She chuckles at that and says now she feels sure she can sleep and wishes him goodnight.

"You're in my thoughts, Judith. Sleep well," Grant replies.

Chapter Twelve

Saturday, February 8, 2020

"Lila, what are you saying? What was Rev Robbie going to do for you?" demands Judith, gripping her friend's arm. Lila turns away saying in a dead and despairing voice:

"It's nothing. Nothing to do with you, and there's nothing you can do. Nobody can do anything. Forget about it."

"But Lila, I want—"

"Look at that," interrupts Lila pointing to the old-style computer set-up on the desk. The monitor and speakers and printer are there, but the CPU is missing. Looking around they discover open desk drawers have been rifled with papers scattered over the chair and floor. The door to the safe is wide open showing an empty interior. The body lies on top of an old-fashioned ledger, as if Rev Robbie has died clutching it to his chest.

Judith notices that one of the man's loafers has been kicked off in his struggles and the sight of that brings her to tears. She is sobbing when Grant arrives. He notices that Lila stands frozen and dry-eyed.

* * * * * *

The police get hold of Mr. Miller to open the auditorium. His precious hardwood is going to get scuffed and marked with everyone traipsing through to be interviewed, but he and his son will deal with that tomorrow. Right now they need to do whatever they can to help the police find Rev Robbie's killer.

Grant appreciates that Patricia Johnson has corralled the volleyball players and their entourage together but wished she'd thought to do the same with the Horticultural Society and the rest of the people in the building. They will eventually figure out who is supposed to be there - and where, who is actually there, and who is missing, but the person with the answers is currently on his way to the morgue.

Grant knew the Reverend Wilcox, although only very casually, and is saddened by his death.

He calls for more personnel to attend the location. They need to gather everyone's name and contact information before releasing anyone. Soon parents are arriving to pick up their teenagers and that adds to the general confusion. Everyone knew Rev Robbie, and everyone is shocked and mournful at his passing.

Inevitably the media pick up some of the tweets and send out reporters and TV crews. The wealthy of Edgemont Village are always news.

At some point someone mentions the opioid Fentanyl. Soon a story of poisoning by drug overdose is circulating. No one believes Rev Robbie was taking recreational drugs but a painkiller? that rumour gets traction. A whole new avenue of investigation opens up.

Calls are placed to Board Members and several descend on the scene brimming with questions and demands. Rich, influential people who are used to getting immediate answers. Grant is relieved when both his boss and his boss's boss present themselves to deal with the upper echelon, and that Suzanne has gone to attach herself to the big brass.

* * * * * *

Andrea Seely joined The Centre's Board as a *Member at Large* waiting until a Director's spot came open. When the position of Treasurer became available she offered to take on that role.

Initially, it seems a much bigger job then she's imagined. The Centre collects membership dues and hosts a lot of activities which require user-fees, wages, services, utilities... until she learns that Rev Robbie takes care of the day-to-day business.

He balances the petty cash, handles the bank deposits, and makes the ledger entries. They also have an accounting firm, working on a pro bono basis, to process payroll, remit taxes, and produce a quarterly financial statement plus file an annual return.

Andrea's job is simply to oversee operations, although she does have to register with the bank for signing authority in case she ever has to deal with one of Rev Robbie's duties.

She enjoys the Board Meetings and likes to use her title when discussing The Centre, hinting at her friendship with Eleanor Frampton and other wealthy townspeople. It also gives her the excuse to spend plenty of time at The Centre, allowing her the pretense of Treasurer business to cover meeting up with Kyle and trying to further their relationship. She only makes a half-hearted effort at secrecy.

Andrea Seely is a flamboyant presence with her brightly coloured clothes cut to flow over her heavy build, and a loud voice matched to a loud laugh. She sees herself as someone to be reckoned with, a very self-satisfied woman.

Now she tries to thrust herself into the police investigation. She announces that as Treasurer it is imperative that she investigate the contents of the safe immediately. Everything is of *the utmost urgency and importance.*

The scene-of-crime staff aren't impressed and refuse to allow the woman into the Reverend's office until they've completed their evidence-gathering. Besides, they already know the safe is empty.

Andrea huffs but her demands are ignored. Finally, she stomps off to vent her complaints to the other board members who are present.

Once the all-clear is given for the ambulance attendants to remove the body Grant goes to find Andrea Seely. She sticks her nose in the air while leading the way back to the office.

First she looks for the petty cash box that resides in the top drawer of the desk during office hours. The box is there, but when she opens it there is nothing inside. No cash, and no vouchers to account for the missing money.

The safe isn't hidden, it sits in a corner of the room and serves as a coffee stand. It doesn't matter if the coffee-maker gets hot, the safe is fireproof, and its surface is resistant to drips and wet spots. The safe sits on a solid base so that anyone opening it won't have to stoop too low to reach inside.

With the door swung open wide it only takes a quick glance to see there are no ledgers or receipt books, and definitely no money inside. The two donation boxes, when opened, prove equally empty of cash although there are several cheques folded inside. There is a sprinkling of some white substance that looks like dust or powder on the floor of the safe, but otherwise it's bare.

Andrea's great show of consulting a note on her phone to get the combination has fallen flat. Now she demands:

"Where are the missing funds?"

Grant schools his face to avoid showing exasperation and begins the painstaking task of asking Andrea Seely question after question trying to get answers.

"How much money was there?"

"Well I don't know, do I?"

"How much do you think should be there?"

"I just said, I don't know."

"Then, how do you know that funds are missing?"

"Of course they're missing, they're not here in the safe where they should be."

"Yes, but how do you know that if you don't know what should be there?"

"Because there has to be something."

"If you don't know how much money should have been in the safe, then you don't know if *any* money *was* in the safe."

"Well of course there was. It's Saturday night, there should be a whole week's worth of collections. The banking is done every Monday morning."

"And how much would a week's worth of collections come to?"

"I don't know. A lot of the money comes in on the weekends... but there's stuff on every night of the week as well. I'm fairly new to the position of Treasurer so I don't have it all at my fingertips just yet."

"Fair enough. We haven't found any ledgers—"

"They would have been kept in the safe," Andrea interrupts.

"Okay, and we can't check the computer—"

Again she interrupts demanding to know why not, pointing to the monitor on the desk. Grant explains that the CPU, the computer's processing unit, is missing. It seems she is about to complain about that as well but settles for pursing her lips and giving him an annoyed look. He feels ready to return it too because sitting in this room absorbing the strong smell of the cloying perfume she wears is making him headachey.

"So we've been robbed, is what you're saying."

"No, I'm not saying that. I have a dead man and indications show he was likely murdered. I have an empty safe and a missing computer but there might be reasonable explanations."

"I doubt that! Like what? No, don't bother to answer, it's obvious to me what's happened: thieves falling out."

"You're accusing Rev Robbie of theft?"

"Who else could it be?

Exasperated Grant retorted: "One possibility is the killer."

"Killer? oh no, he must have committed suicide."

Grant bites back the urge to snap *oh is that likely?* and instead settles for raising an eyebrow. Andrea Seely hurries to add:

"He probably figured he was about to get caught for the stealing and took this way out."

"So then where is the money?"

"Well I don't know. Stashed away somewhere."

Grant appears to consider this then replies mildly:

"So your theory is that Rev Robbie stole the money from the safe, took it somewhere for safekeeping, then returned to this very room to kill himself. Have I got that right, Ms. Seely?"

"Oh honestly, you can't expect me to do your job for you," she huffs before flouncing out of the room. Grant watches with interest having never known exactly what flouncing meant before.

Chapter Thirteen

Sunday, February 9, 2020

Judith doesn't get out of bed until late but she hasn't enjoyed a refreshing sleep. Not surprising with the shock of Rev Robbie's death and afterwards having to hang around waiting around to be interviewed.

Then, once she does get home, it's difficult to fall asleep. Plenty of thoughts about the killing, the method, Lila's concern – to name a few – chase round her head as she lies in bed. And of course Grant's involvement. In the few moments they spent together she can tell he is preoccupied and eager to get started.

Grant hurriedly explains that it appears to be a poisoning death but they don't know yet how it the poison was taken. Accidentally? or deliberately, and if so, by whose hand? Even once the method is confirmed they still won't know those answers. He has a difficult task ahead of him, especially since the victim is so well-loved. No one has a motive.

She gets dressed, eventually, and makes herself look presentable on the off-chance that Grant might stop by. She isn't surprised when he doesn't, certain he will be extremely busy.

After a couple of attempts to reach Lila by phone and by text Judith gives up. Time weighs heavily on her and although Sundays have always been a stress-free, relaxing day in the past today feels like it's dragging on and on.

* * * * * *

When Pat Johnson finishes loading up the dishwasher she's tempted to switch it on but knows she'll hear about that from her husband. Ever since Mark retired he's taken a critical interest in how the household is run, and complains if any of the appliances are used unless they're as full as possible.

He checks over the utility bills to make sure they are consistent with the previous month. If the electric bill is really high he'll dig out his copies from the year before and compare. He is always on the look-out for a power drain or, in the case of the water bill, a leak that is running up costs.

Both he and Pat are shocked and upset about Rev Robbie's death, especially since both of them were there at the time. They figure out when they had last seen and last spoken to Rev Robbie then each sits quietly for a moment remembering the man.

"I wonder who will take his funeral service?" muses Pat. "It won't be the reverend who replaced him, surely it will be someone higher up."

"I really don't know. Haven't given it any thought. Actually, sad as I am about Rev Robbie, I have to confess I was really interested in what Jim Henley was telling me about his collection of cacti. Someone gave him a Christmas cactus for a gift and did you know that these plants are completely different from most cacti?

Also there are Easter and Thanksgiving versions, too All flowering. Anyhow, he's giving me a cutting and tells me I'll have no trouble growing my own cactus that can easily last for decades! I was reading about it online just before we had lunch and I'm looking forward to giving it a try."

Pat agrees that flowering cacti will be very nice during the winter months but inside she longs to gossip about Rev Robbie's death. Mark never has any interest in speculation, he's all about facts and truths, but she likes to ponder the how, why and, who behind the mystery. And she really likes to have a good chat with a like-minded friend.

She has no idea what Judith Taylor does on her days off but decides that under this circumstance, and their mutual feeling for Rev Robbie, that she is justified in phoning for a gossip. Judith answers her phone on the first ring and is delighted that Pat has called.

They discuss their suspicions and theories about Rev Robbie's death then Judith says:

"I'm concerned about Lila. As you know she discovered Rev Robbie's body first when we went into his office at The Centre–"

"I was glad to see the two of you together last night because I know there'd been some sort of falling out or whatever..." Pat's words trail away but the interest in her voice encourages Judith to elaborate.

"Oh Pat, it's been awful. Lila and I weren't at The Centre together, we met up after having both travelled there separately although I'd offered to bring her.

She and I have barely spoken in the past five weeks. Ever since her estranged husband came to town for a weekend. We were all supposed to get together while he was here but then but she cancelled. She refuses to discuss Arnie's visit at all. Whatever happened has upset her deeply and then there was last night's gruesome discovery. And she was so close to him, too."

"Oh I am disappointed to hear that, Judith. It's been a real pleasure for me to see you two getting on so well. I mean, and I know you won't mind me saying this, you aren't the easiest person to get along with. I like you just as you are and have no problem, neither does Mark, neither does Eleanor Frampton! but I know some of the teaching staff gets on your nerves and, well, they aren't happy when you won't join in on their various functions. At least they weren't, I thought I'd seen a lot more friendliness from the teachers lately."

"That's true, and you've got some good teachers who are dedicated to their jobs. The one or two bad apples can only exert so much influence. The rest are now standing up for themselves."

"So you've been a good influence on them and Lila's been a good influence on you."

"She really has. I just wish I could be as good a friend to her as she's been to me."

"Oh, I'm sure you are—"

"But Pat, even Rev Robbie spoke to me about Lila and how I should be pushing her to talk. I told him I'd tried but he just said *'try harder'* and I didn't."

"Oh Judith, I'm sure things will work out. We just have to be patient and give it time."

* * * * * *

Lila's phone is blowing up with texts and phone-calls. She doesn't answer any of them. People are morbidly curious about the finding of the body, wanting to know what she saw, and how it made her feel. At moment's like this Lila feels like shunning the entire human race.

When she hears the thump-thump of her landlady's cane on the floor above Lila hurries upstairs. She isn't in the mood for company, but there is always the chance that her elderly neighbour is in difficulty and needs Lila's help as a neighbour or even as a professional nurse.

Still wearing her pyjamas she comes through the door inside Mrs. P's kitchen and inhales deeply, enjoying the sugar and vanilla smells of home baking. Fortunately the spry old lady is fine, just concerned about her tenant, and has wrapped up a dozen cookies as comfort food for her. Hiding her reluctance Lila agrees to stay for the kindly offered cup of tea.

Mrs. Piernitsky isn't fooled but she pretends not to notice Lila's lack of enthusiasm, knowing that half-an-hour spent consuming a hot drink and a slice of freshly baked cake will do the younger woman a world of good. She is very fond of Lila and had been prepared to like her husband too, but she saw very little of him and can't form an opinion. The landlady is very deaf and totally unaware of the yelling that has gone on in the basement of her home during Arnie's weekend visit the month before.

Chapter Fourteen

Tuesday, February 11, 2020

Valentine's Day is coming up and Grant's partner, Suzanne Mirteau, has been making snide remarks all day. Suzanne, despite all she has in good looks, brains, and skills, lacks self-confidence. It seems she measures her worth by the degree of interest shown by the men around her.

Grant thinks highly of Suzanne as a co-worker – and his safety depends on her as his partner in law enforcement – but he isn't attracted, and she won't or can't accept that.

She was flirtatious and possessive before he met Judith Taylor, but now her jealousy is almost out-of-control. Grant is seriously considering requesting a change of partner and only hesitates because as the senior officer it won't reflect well on Suzanne who he knows is ambitious.

He's spent the day ignoring the nasty comments which he's sure will be even worse tomorrow. He's even thought of sending Suzanne an anonymous bouquet from *A Secret Admirer* just to keep her happy but decided against shelling out for the inflated cost of Valentine's Day flowers. He isn't planning to send flowers to Judith so why would he spend money on Suzanne?

He lets his mind drift to thoughts of Judith. She'd looked very pretty and he was flattered she'd dressed up for her dinner date with him on Saturday night. Quite a contrast to the well-worn clothes she had on when they went to the show. The small smile that plays around his lips while he reminisces serves to infuriate his angry partner even more.

He is surprised – and secretly pleased – when Suzanne suddenly blurts out that she's being reassigned, at her request, to the opioid task force.

"I won't bother asking if you'd like to go out for a farewell drink in case your girlfriend gets jealous," she says with a sneer that turns her beautiful face ugly.

Grant recoils slightly from the anger in her eyes before calmly replying:

"I'm sure it won't be goodbye, Suzanne. In fact, I expect your investigation will overlap with the Rev Robbie murder now that the lab has confirmed the cause of death iss, as suspected, an overdose of Fentanyl."

* * * * * *

In a phone-call later that afternoon he passes on the news about Suzanne's departmental change to Judith.

"I have to admit that I'm glad I won't be seeing or talking to Suzanne anymore. She's never hid her dislike or contempt for me, and I still don't know what I did to rub her the wrong way," confides Judith in reply. Grant is quite sure the problem has nothing to do with Judith herself, but with Grant's attraction to her.

"Suzanne is a very good police officer except she's got a blind spot when it comes to self-appraisal. She's narcissistic and vain, and quick to take offence at any perceived slight. It took me a long time to see this. I used to ignore her come-ons but finally had to out-and-out reject her when her antics interfered with our work. She seemed to accept that until I met you. Once she realized I wasn't going to *come to my senses* as she put it – she turned nasty. So long as she gets her own way everything is rosy but boy she sure is a trial to work with when she's been thwarted."

"So her transfer is a relief to you as well?"

"It is. I don't care if my next partner is male or female but I sure do hope they're happily married!"

"It must be difficult being married to a police officer... I mean, the hours and worrying about their safety."

"It's one of many jobs where there is risk involved: firefighters, military personnel, EMTs, construction workers... even someone doing a routine job like meter-reading could be in danger from a gas leak explosion. Tragically, schools have been venues for deadly violence, too."

"Every time we hear about a school shooting it just terrifies all of us."

"Unfortunately it's the very strong taboo of harming defenceless innocents that attracts the biggest headlines. From what I've learned the shooter is often an ex-student exacting revenge – of real or just perceived threats or attacks – but schools have become the target of thrill killers as well. It is a very scary situation."

"So you're saying any marriage could face career issues – even dangers?"

"Hmm, yes, but for example I've been a cop for seventeen, no it's eighteen years now, and I've never been shot at.

Anyhow, with Suzanne gone and no new partner assigned yet I was hoping you could be my sounding-board since I trust your discretion and judgement."

"I'm flattered," Judith replies, and he smiles at hearing the seriousness of her tone.

Chapter Fifteen

Wednesday, February 12, 2020

It is unseasonably mild and sunny when Grant drops in at the school just as Judith is finishing up.

"This is a nice surprise!" she exclaims. Grant gives a crooked smile and tells her she is to be his antidote to a rotten turn of events.

"I thought we could go for a walk. It won't be dark for another 45 minutes or so and it's so nice to see the sun."

"That's a great idea. In fact, I walked to school today because it was 7 C when I was ready to come to work so at the last moment I decided to leave the car behind."

"Perfect, that means you'll have walking shoes. In fact that sweater and pants outfit looks perfect for a brisk outing, it uh, fits you very well."

Judith is wearing a Nordic-patterned sweater in white/green/blue with matching navy slacks. She usually wears pants to work in the winter time.

"Thank you! I don't wear the sweater often because it's quite warm but it will be perfect for a hike."

"How about this then: we'll drive to Picnic Hill but we'll avoid the off-leash dog park and wander along one of the trails until the sun starts to set. By then we'll probably feel a bit chilly so I'll take you back to my place for a hot chocolate in front of the fireplace. Sound good?"

"You've got a fireplace? Lucky you!" Judith says with enthusiasm adding, "Let's go, you can tell me about your rotten day and get it off your chest."

"I'll wait till we're out walking," replies Grant, opening the front door to lead her out to the parking lot. They both spot Lila at the same time and Grant waves while Judith calls out to her but Lila just gives a quick wave back and hurries into her car.

"Still no word from her, eh?"

"Nothing. She's always just like that – polite-friendly rather than friend-friendly. It's been going on like this for weeks." Judith is unhappy, but also resigned to the new reality of her relationship with Lila.

"She's on my list to be re-interviewed. I'm not looking forward to it but I should get it taken care of sooner rather than later, I guess."

Neither one says much on the drive to Picnic Hill, so called because it's a local beauty spot that serves families, lovers, and pet owners. Edgemont School for Girls frequently organizes science class trips to study nature during the different seasons there so Judith knows her way around the area quite well.

After he parks the car Judith leads Grant to the far left pathway which she says is an easy 25- to 30-minute walk that circles back to their starting point.

The walking paths have been cleared of snow by the volunteers from various service clubs who take turns looking after Picnic Hill. That usually means cleaning up the messes left by human visitors, but also keeping the pathways free.

"So what happened to ruin your day?" asks Judith once they get walking at a good pace.

"I had a likely lead to pursue, I'll tell you the backstory in a minute, and it took ages to track down the person in question only to have him alibi up right away. I didn't realize how much I was counting on this being the solution and now I've been let down hard. Serves me right because I have to admit this never felt right in my gut but I ignored that. Anyhow, the story is..."

Judith draws closer so she won't miss a thing. Grant has a knack with words that make his interviews come alive. They slow down a bit and he tucks her arm into his, holding her close to his side.

"Rev Robbie's wife Peg – Margaret, actually – died a year ago September. They'd been married for a very long time and everyone felt so sorry for him having to live on his own without her. Everyone, that is, except for her brother Matthew.

Matthew is still working, he's about 12 years younger than Peg was, and he's in sales and boy, so difficult to pin down for a meeting. Just to talk first of all, because my lead was based on hearsay, not actual evidence, but he just wouldn't make himself available. So of course I started wondering if he was avoiding me and if he had a good reason to do so. A good, guilty reason. However that's not how things turned out.

I got onto Matthew from a neighbour of Peg and Rev Robbie's, another one called Margaret, who was the oldest of them all. She's frail, but her mind is still sharp and she said Matthew had accused Rev Robbie of killing Peg and then proceeded to threaten he'd *get him*.

Apparently Peg had been in charge of Matthew's raising for much of his life so he'd gotten used to being spoiled by her. But once she got married to Rev Robbie Matthew lost all that special attention and, according to this Margaret, was bitterly jealous for the entire fifty-year's of his sister's marriage! Can you imagine?"

"I can't imagine being married for fifty years?"

"No?"

"Well, that's the Golden Wedding Anniversary, right? You don't hear about very many of those."

Grant's voice lowers to a murmur when he says: "I could imagine fifty years – with the right woman, that is."

At his words, said in such a confiding tone, Judith feels a little shiver of pleasure ripple through her body but hopes her down-filled jacket hides it. Grant correctly interprets the movement he feels coming from her, but gives no indication.

"Anyhow, the brother never specified exactly how Rev Robbie was supposed to have killed Peg, I think she died of a stroke, but he kicked off at the funeral, at the burial site, and again in the Church's social room where they served refreshments afterwards.

Margaret said he made an awful fool out of himself and that Rev Robbie, his brother-in-law, tried to calm Matthew down but it was no use. He just shouted out his threats of vengeance, warning Rev Robbie that he'd *get him* no matter how long it took.

So, he sounds like a pretty good suspect, right? certainly worth a chat. Then, when I realized he was dodging my calls I really thought I was on to something. When I finally got hold of him at his work and managed to pin him down to a time and place he was a no-show.

So, now I was really thinking this guy was trying to hide something. And he was but, talk about ridiculous: he was avoiding me because he thought I was after him for driving with an expired driver's licence. I mean, how would I even know that? how would anyone know something like that? but it was his guilty conscience.

I'm investigating a suspicious death that's probably a homicide and this guy is dodging me because of traffic tickets? What a waste of time.

Turns out he has several speeding tickets, a couple of red-light camera tickets, and *a shitload of parking tickets* as he put it. Well you might not know this but here in Alberta you can't renew your driver's licence or your provincial plates if you've got outstanding fines. So he's been driving without a valid licence, but to make matters worse because he knew that his insurance would go up because of demerits for tickets and fines he let that lapse as well.

So here's this guy in his late fifties or early sixties driving around with no licence and no insurance. His $1,000 worth of fines has just jumped up an additional $4,000 or so.

Anyhow, I was so angry at him wasting my time with his foolishness I reported his licence plate to Traffic and he'll get stopped unless he's smart enough to have cabbed it straight to a Registry office today to get paid up."

Grant shakes his head in disgust but Judith can't help letting a giggle escape, explaining:

"It's so anti-climactic."

Grant chuckles and quipped: "And that's always frustrating."

"Oh good one!" laughs Judith.

* * * * * *

Grant's apartment is brand-new and built over the homeowner's garage. It's done up in shades of gray accented with black. Even the bathroom fixtures are black. All the appliances are brushed stainless steel, and the counters are marble. It's very modern, very masculine-looking, and stops just short of being cold and sterile.

Both Judith and Grant agree that a wood-burning fireplace would be cozier but the gas fire lights up instantly at the flick of a switch. Having no wood to bring in, or ashes to take out, is a convenient bonus.

Grant's living-room furniture consists of oxblood leather seating, Mission-style tables, and he has a few big Hudson's Bay signature striped cushions adding colour. Judith pushes a couple of them onto the floor and sits on one with her back resting against the couch and her feet warming by the fire.

When Grant comes in with their drinks on a tray he pauses to admire how relaxed she looks, and how pretty in the glow of firelight. He sets the tray on the coffee-table then slides down onto the other cushion. Taking her in his arms he gives her a tight squeeze and covers her face with kisses.

"That tickles!" she cries pulling back with a smile. They stare into each other's eyes for a long moment before meeting in a deep, satisfying kiss.

The marshmallows have melted into the hot chocolate - that is no longer hot but still chocolatey and delicious - when they finally came up for air.

Chapter Sixteen

Thursday, February 13, 2020

As things turn out Grant is able to interview Lila the next day. They meet in her nurse's office at the school and he is shocked at how she has changed from a happy, vibrant woman to someone who is despairing and despondent. Her hair needs washing and the shadows under her eyes speak of too many sleepless nights in a row.

She sits slumped in her chair while he starts off with a few work-related questions to put her at her ease:

"I understand that your job at The Centre is a volunteer position to deal with potential injuries during sporting events?"

Lila nods.

"Anything else?"

"I've given first aid a few times."

"Can you give me some examples?"

She sighs deeply then slowly answers:

"Once when an art instructor cut her fingers quite badly with an X-Acto blade, and another time a girl fainted... but I don't remember why."

"And how well did you know Rev Robbie?"

"Really well, and I just loved him and I miss him so much! For the first time Lila's voice became animated. "When I'm at The Centre it's always with the hope that my professional skills won't be needed so I spent a lot of time talking with him. He was a wonderfully kind and caring man. He had a great sense of humour, too."

"Did you work alongside him at all, by that I mean in his bookkeeping work for The Centre?"

"Well, we spent time in his office and he'd be working then. Is that what you mean?"

"Actually, Lila, I'm trying to get a clearer picture of Rev Robbie's day-to-day activities. I know he handled the bank deposits for The Centre's donations, and monies collected from refreshment sales, and collection boxes. All the funds that were paid the week prior to his death are missing, and there were only a few cheques in the safe. Someone said he always did the banking on Monday mornings, would you say he was regular in his habits?"

Lila take so long in answering that Grant wonders if she is going to do so. He's just about to prompt her when she finally says:

"Is someone accusing him of something? How could they? that's just... oh, what does it matter now, anyway? He's gone, and... sure he was a stickler for routine but so what?"

"Lila, I have a very unprofessional urge to offer you a shoulder to cry on! I'm very sorry you've lost your friend and I know, when you feel a bit better, it will be important to you that I find out what happened.

Meanwhile, I'll reschedule this re-interview for another time. Let me know if there's anything I can do. And you must know the same goes for Judith, too. Please, take care of yourself, okay?"

"I'm sorry, Grant. I'm in a bit of a fog and I can't seem to get my head clear. Yes, please, let's finish this another time."

He gives her a small smile and leaves.

Driving away from the school Grant can't stop thinking about the dramatic change in Lila. He knows she's struggling with a problem in her personal life, as well as losing Rev Robbie, so she's had to deal with a lot of sad, pressured, and stressful situations in a short time.

"I hope she and Judith can repair their friendship because if anyone needs a friend right now that person is Lila Morelli," he thinks sadly. "Especially since she's the one who discovered his body."

That makes him consider the logistics more closely:

"Why *did* the murder happen when it was likely to be discovered right away? there was a huge risk of being caught so what forced the killer to act so precipitously?"

Chapter Seventeen

Friday, February 14, 2020

The student's are excited to exchange St Valentine's Day cards at the school. Edgemont's policy is that anyone who wants to give out valentines has to give to everyone in their home-room class. The local card shops don't have a lot of variety to choose from in their card packs so each student seems to be carrying several identical cards.

There are about three dozen of them on Judith's desk. Last year – and every year before that – she'd received none. This year every card she opens gives her a pleasant-feeling pang in her heart.

She's been hoping she'll be able to see Grant for awhile this evening. They aren't going to go out, they've just planned on spending some time at her place.

Judith understands that making plans during an investigation is tricky so she is baking a dessert for him as a Valentine treat. It's especially sad that it is Rev Robbie's murder that might prevent him from getting away.

Judith had spent almost an hour reading the verse inside every single valentine card in the store before finally settling on something that fell far short of what she wanted to say, but at least didn't make any assumptions – or promises.

Some of the cards had sentimental wording that was way over the top, some so-called funny cards were downright insulting, and it seemed like 90% were addressed to "My Adorable Husband" or "My Darling Wife".

Judith sighed over her choice of a friendship card but really, that was the most suitable option.

She's forgotten to pack a lunch today so she decides to go check up on Lila. Maybe she'd like to go out for lunch or would appreciate having something brought in? Judith takes her purse out of the desk drawer and heads to the Nurse's Office only to discover Lila has phoned in sick today. Judith puzzles over that since Lila hadn't been sick yesterday.

Grant had told her about his failed interview though, so maybe Lila has taken his advice and is catching up on sleep and getting a good rest.

Judith tells herself: "I'll go over to her place now and see if she needs anything."

Always happiest when she has a firm plan in mind she fetches her outdoor things from the staff-room and heads out to her car in the parking-lot. Unfortunately her plan gets derailed when she sees the shattered glass from one of the back-seat windows of her sedan. The window has been smashed and the pile of ledgers and manilla folders that she'd gotten earlier from Rev Robbie are missing.

Judith is glad, for the millionth time it seems, that Suzanne Mirteau is no longer working alongside Grant. She could just imagine that bad-tempered police officer's sneer at the idea of Judith calling Grant because her car got vandalized.

Except this isn't so much about the damage to her car as the content of the stolen articles. Judith is quite sure Grant will be interested in the theft of the murder victim's files.

* * * * * *

Grant has dispatched a patrol car to come by the school. The two officers have taken photos of the broken window and written down

Judith's statement. They give her a copy of the report explaining she'll need it for her insurance company.

"Oh, it's just a side window. I expect it will cost way less than my deductible to replace."

The officers exchange a look and one answers Judith saying:

"That window will probably cost about $650 to replace, maybe more, depends on the hourly rate for labour."

Judith is shocked at the estimate and says so but the officers just shrug it off, telling her she's lucky the thief didn't damage the car door or she'd be replacing much more and at a higher cost.

She just shakes her head at that. Confirming that it's okay for her to drive her car, she then thanks the two officers for coming out so promptly.

"Oh a friend of the boss will always get prompt service," says one of the young men with a cheeky grin. He winks at his partner but Judith's expressionless face makes him think twice about adding any further remarks.

When Judith had first phoned Grant he'd told her that he definitely planned to keep their coffee date tonight although he might be late arriving and unable to stay for very long. When she sees him she'll ask about how the officers know she is his friend. She doesn't want to get anyone in trouble, but she does want an answer.

She sorts through her feelings for a moment trying to make up her mind whether or not she is flattered or offended that people are linking her and Grant as *friends*.

Then she gives a little smile and decides she likes the idea, hoping the young police officers aren't this very minute wondering what it is that

Grant sees in her. She would blush if she could hear what they are saying.

Chapter Eighteen

Friday, February 14, 2020

Judith turns back into the school searching for Mr. Glover, the school's caretaker and custodian of all the keys. He is an older man, probably past the usual retirement age, who is always on hand to help out.

After wandering from one end of the building to the other Judith finally finds him in her own office, cleaning the inside of the windows.

The most striking thing about Mr. Glover is his extremely bushy eyebrows with bristly hairs jutting straight out. His eyeglasses always sit low on his nose as if the frames have been pushed down.

"Oh Mr. Glover, hello! I have another job for you that might not wait until you're done here, and I'm afraid this one's outdoors. Someone's smashed my car window and there's shattered glass in the parking-lot, it's quite dangerous."

The old man stows his window-cleaning supplies neatly until he can return and quizzes Judith about the damage, tut-tutting over such vandalism.

"If you can wait a moment I'll just get my broom and a bin for that glass then you can point me in the right direction. No point you coming outside in this chill wind."

"Oh, I've got to find some cardboard or something I can put over the open window because, as you say, it is windy and cold."

"I'll take care of that for you, don't you worry about it."

"Oh no, Mr. Glover, fixing up my car's broken window isn't part of your duties for the school, I'll take care..."

"Never you mind, Miss Judith. Miss Patricia will read me the riot act and take a strip off my hide if I don't help out a damsel in distress. Especially when the trouble occurred on school property."

When Judith felt he'd run through his repertoire of applicable cliches she gave him sincere thanks and pointed through her office window to her car, the wine-colored Subaru.

"Ah, that foreign car. Bigger than most of them are. And it's supposed to be good for winter driving too, eh?"

"Yes, all Subarus come with four-wheel drive. Of course I still put on winter snow tires because well... no one wants to get stuck waiting on a tow-truck in miserable weather."

"Yup, you need snow tires or chains for Alberta winters. Well, you just sit tight and I'll let you know when you're good to go."

"Actually, I'll be in the principal's office, I need to get some cheques signed. Thank you very much for your help, Mr. Glover."

He tips his hat and heads off to work on this new task, which is much more interesting than window-cleaning.

Judith gathers up a couple of file folders and heads out of the Library to see Principal Johnson.

* * * * * *

An hour later Judith is in her car heading to Lila's. Wind protection in the form of cardboard securely taped has been applied by the janitor and Judith tipped him with a book of Tim Horton's coupons. Mr. Glover is delighted. She knows cash wouldn't have been accepted, but honestly can't see the difference.

After getting Pat's signature alongside her own on a number of cheques from the school's two accounts Judith tucks her reading glasses back into their case and asks for permission to leave early.

"Oh by all means, that's rotten luck about the vandalism to your car. Unless it was kids throwing rocks or something?"

"No, this wasn't vandalism, I was robbed."

"What?!"

"Well, not me personally. I had a couple of ledgers and files from Rev Robbie's office at The Centre. He'd given them to me a couple of days ago, did you know I was helping him balance the books? anyhow, I hadn't carried them up to my apartment yet. Entirely my fault and I feel badly about it but yeah, that's what was stolen from the backseat of my car."

"Files and ledgers don't sound valuable, certainly not to a casual thief."

"No, you're right. That's why I put a call into Detective Grant. I think it must be connected to Rev Robbie's murder."

"They're certain it was murder? or can't you say?"

"No, I misspoke. The police are certain it was poison but they can't tell, or at least won't tell me, how it was administered. Right now it's still a suspicious death but that just means it could be an accident, a suicide, or murder."

"I don't see how it could be an accident except that it must be. Suicide is out of the question, and Rev Robbie was a lovely man, no one could possibly want to do him harm."

"I agree except... he was tough. If he was on the track of some wrongdoing I'm sure he would pursue it and maybe that frightened someone."

"Oh Judith. What a sorry mess. Anyhow, by all means you can leave now, see to your car or just go home and relax with your feet up and a cup of tea."

"That sounds wonderful but actually, I'm really getting concerned about Lila. So, although she's been giving me the cold-shoulder if she's home sick I think I should check in, see if she needs anything."

"By all means, go to her place and tell her I've officially sanctioned the visit and want to see things resolved between the two of you."

"Hmm, not sure how well Lila Morelli will bow to authority–"

"Oh goodness, nobody's scared of me except the parents and that's only because they don't want their little darlings sent home to be in their care all day!"

The two women share a chuckle and Judith packs up her files. She returns her work to her own office, locks up her desk, and grabs her winter coat from the chair where she'd dropped it an hour before, then heads out to her car. All the glass has been swept away, and the parking-lot is now safe for drivers and the tires of their cars.

* * * * * *

Lila isn't pleased when she answers the door but she doesn't want Mrs. Piernitsky, her elderly landlady, to hear an argument so she invites Judith in.

Lila is wearing a track suit, her hair is a tousled mess, and her eyes red-rimmed. Judith can't tell if the marks indicate lack of sleep or a bout of crying. The whole dishevelled look – so unlike her friend – makes Judith blink back tears herself. When Lila sees and feels Judith's true caring emotion her face crumples and she bends her head sobbing. Judith gathers her into an embrace and hugs tight.

Moments later they are on the couch, holding each other's hands, and both talking, explaining, apologizing, and finally laughing together. Judith is so relieved.

"I guess we, or rather I, do need to talk. I owe you the truth, Judith. It just isn't easy."

"Well, let's talk over food. I haven't eaten since breakfast and I'm starved. We'll get a delivery of what? chicken or Chinese or pizza or? What do you feel like?"

Before Lila can answer there is a thump-thump noise on the ceiling.

"That's Mrs. P banging on her floor. Give me a second to just check on her." Lila hurries upstairs from her basement suite and Judith is just beginning to worry when she hears her friend clattering back down the stairs calling:

"Thanks again, it smells divine!"

Lila comes into the room bearing a large pot of fragrant homemade chicken noodle soup. She explains that Mrs. P made it because she thought Lila was sick. Lila has told her that she's just unhappy about the death of her friend, Rev Robbie, but the old lady presses it on her saying she needs building up.

"It's making my mouth water!" exclaims Judith breathing in the aroma and checking out the flat noodles and juicy chunks of chicken. She helps by setting out bowls and cutlery while Lila fetches some crusty rolls.

"Butter?" asks Judith.

"Oh right, I always forget you don't eat your bread like an Italian."

"This is delicious soup!"

"She's a wonderful cook and I'm so lucky to live here," Lila lifts a brimming spoon and says: "Cheers!"

"Happy St. Valentine's Day," returns Judith.

"Don't remind me about that, I'll start bawling again. Oh wait, don't you have plans with Grant?"

"I texted and cancelled when you were upstairs. It's more important that I spend time with you right now."

"Oh shut-up or I will lose it."

"That's okay, that's what friends are for."

The two exchange happy smiles then delay their conversation until after finishing their meal.

Chapter Nineteen

Friday, February 14, 2020

After tidying up from their meal the two women go into the living-room area. Judith sits down on the sofa but instead of joining her Lila moves to the armchair.

"This is going to be a difficult conversation," she begins. Reaching for the box of tissues she holds it in her lap. "I don't think I have any tears left but I say that every day and then surprise myself."

Judith leans forward, her face full of sympathy, waiting for Lila to find the words.

"I expect you've been thinking up all kinds of things, maybe speculating with Grant—"

"I tried to because, well as you know I'm pretty new to this friendship thing, but he wouldn't play along. Stubborn man. But Lila, just come right out and tell me what happened. Just say whatever it is fast, like ripping off a bandage."

"You're right. There's no point beating around the bush. You wouldn't be able to guess, not in a million years, so dragging this out is just stupid. Okay, here goes:

Arnie has committed a very serious crime and he's gotten away with it. But, it nagged at him until he was no longer himself which is what caused the rift between us. Now that he's told me he wants me to help him cover it up. I don't *think* I can do that, but I *know* I can't betray him. But I also know I should."

Judith's mouth drops open. Lila is right, she would never have guessed at something like this. This is so much worse than an affair.

"He's making you an accessory."

"And now that you've dragged it out of me you are, too. Unless we stop right here. If you can forget what I just said then I can as well. There's no need to involve you further, Judith. You know what kind of a problem I'm dealing with, and you know that I have to resolve it on my own. It would be great to have you play Devil's Advocate but I love you my friend, and that means I love you too much to put you in this position."

"Oh Lila, I don't know what to say. Of course I'm here to listen to you. Accessory? I'm not even sure if that applies. This is Alberta and the incident occurred in Ontario, right?"

"It's not an incident, it's a crime. It's the crime of... manslaughter, I think. It was an accident but it wasn't reported so I think that escalates it from unlawful killing, or something like that, to manslaughter. Probably involuntary manslaughter? Oh, I don't know, it's a goddamn mess!"

Judith is sitting stunned, her face white as she asks:

"Somebody died?"

Lila hurries over to sit on the couch and takes Judith's hand.

"I'm sorry, I've lived with this for weeks and forgot how deeply shocked I was when I first heard about it. Oh Judith, it's awful, I know."

"What exactly happened?"

"Are you sure you want me to tell you?"

"Oh, we're well past that point now, Lila. I mean, somebody *died*."

"An old lady, although that doesn't make it any better of course. Here's the story that Arnie told me:

It was in the morning and he was out working his usual route. The garbage trucks drive one way down the street picking up the bins, and then they turn around and come back up the same street doing the other side of the road.

Here in Edgemont this all happens in the back alleys but in Toronto the bins are mostly put out at the end of people's driveways on the road. But there are some alleys too, and it was in one of them that this happened.

The alleys are usually behind commercial or multi-residential, like apartment buildings, and most businesses pay for private garbage collection so the alley runs are pretty quick.

Well, he has no idea how it happened but I'm sure he was wearing his headphones and unable to hear a cry or anything like that, and, of course, slightly high so not as alert as he should have been."

"Slightly high?" interrupts Judith.

"Actually yeah, because Arnie is a habitual user and I don't mean daily I mean several times a day. He's in a constant state of high and has developed a tolerance. If it wasn't for the stinkweed smell you probably wouldn't be able to tell. He takes a few tokes, gets a buzz, goes about his merry way. Functioning. Some alcoholics are like that too, and often no one knows until they sober up and then you see the difference.

So, he's driving along one side of the alley and from the corner of his eye he sees a person, no idea if it's a man or a woman, approaching the truck. They aren't trying to get his attention, not waving their arms or anything so he doesn't think anything of it. He stops to grab a bin, I think the mechanical arms only take about 30 seconds to hook up, lift, dump, then replace the emptied bin back down, so he's only been stopped for about half a minute and no one has crossed in front of him. He thinks he might have possibly felt the tires bump over something maybe – that's how he described the event – but he isn't sure, and he doesn't stop. Instead, he continues to the end of the alley, crosses a road, picks up at the next alley, crosses another road then picks up at the last alley, before turning around to repeat the process in reverse.

By time he gets back to do the other side of the first alley he sees it's now blocked by a police car, and an ambulance, but its lights aren't flashing.

A couple of people are standing watching the paramedics picking up a person huddled on the ground. There's no urgency in their movements so he knows right away the victim is dead. At least, that's what Arnie said.

He isn't too worried about the cops smelling weed on him because people expect the garbage truck and its driver to smell, plus he keeps a tin of coffee grounds in the cab which work well to absorb the odor. So he gets out of the truck but the police just shoo him away saying they need to preserve the scene in the hopes of finding evidence of the hit-and-run vehicle.

So he backs out of the alley, reports back at the depot why he couldn't finish his collection and like Chesterton's postman no one notices him so he got away with it."

"That's just an incredible story," says Judith quietly.

"I know, eh? So anyhow, turns out the victim is a elderly woman but they don't know exactly how old she was, in fact they don't know much about her at all. She's homeless and, according to the newspaper, she's known at a local shelter as Betty.

She's been in the area for years, people know her by sight, and give her change, but she doesn't go around begging, she scavenges for recyclables and turns them in at the bottle depot. The folks at the homeless shelter say she never causes any trouble, obeys all their rules, and doesn't seem to have any particular friends."

"Sad life, sad death."

"Oh, don't..."

"Sorry."

They both sit there with sad faces thinking about the victim and about themselves. Then Judith sits up straight saying:

"So, now... what happens now? Do you move back to Toronto? back to your old job? back to your marriage?"

"No, none of those things. Arnie says he wants to keep our marriage, that he still loves me and I'm the only woman for him, but I told him flat out we're done. That can't – won't – change. I no longer love him and it's because of him, it's his actions that destroyed the feelings I once had.

I realize that seems to have happened really quickly, but you know, we'd been together for so long that our love has probably been more from habit than from being *in love*. But it was always enough for me.

I mean, having children would have made it better, but the kids would have come along in time. There's an old song by Alice Cooper, believe it or not, about a couple living a life *of bed and TV being enough for a working man*, and that's always felt right to me, too.

I'm never going to attend a Gala Movie Premiere or some swanky Art Gallery's Grand Opening, I won't ever be filthy rich or famous, and that's okay. I'm okay with just enjoying a comfortable and hmm, unexciting life. Not boring, because I'm almost never bored, but happy.

Not the 'happily ever after' of a fairy tale but, well, when we did make love it was pretty damn hot and fun, too. I'm gonna miss that. I do miss that, when he was here we did it right away, but after what he told me? no way."

"It's so unfair, Lila. You did nothing wrong but you're sharing the punishment."

"Yeah, well punishment is the issue, actually. What am I going to do about Arnie?"

"I don't think you have a choice, really. You have to get him to turn himself in, otherwise it will eat away at you, the way it's haunted Arnie."

"Believe me I tried! He wouldn't come to dinner on a double-date with you and Grant when he found out Grant was a cop. He couldn't keep the secret any longer but begged me not to tell anyone. I told him I needed to think about that and that's what I was still doing when you ambushed me today."

"Then you'll have to be the one to tell his secret."

"Huh! To my family? They're cops. That's why he wouldn't spend Christmas with them, he's got a guilty conscience."

"Does he? because wouldn't he turn himself in if he did? I mean, wouldn't he have it pretty easy – easier than most, anyways – if he confessed to his in-laws and had their help to guide him through the system?"

"I think that ship has sailed, months ago. He had a chance to do the right thing but he deliberately chose not to. And of course it hasn't helped that the victim is a lonely bag lady with no one to push the cops for a solution. I'm sure they'd like to nab her killer, but time and resources being what they are well..."

"So he's feeling secure, wants to sweep it all under the rug – in fact he tried to do so, tried to pretend that nothing happened and nothing was wrong. You leaving him forced him to address the problem. Then he eased his burden by dumping half of it on your shoulders."

"Just like I've done to you. And just like I pushed him to confide, you forced me. Now we're all miserable!"

"Hopefully we can find a way to fix this. I'll ask Grant about jurisdiction–"

"Oh God Judith, no! You can't tell Grant about this! Just like I can't say anything to my family. You and I can get in trouble for knowing but cops? they'd be forced to act or else be complicit. No, no, no! You can not breathe a word of this."

Lila has gotten quite agitated so Judith calms her friend by agreeing to keep the secret between the two of them.

"But what am I going to tell him? He likes you, Lila, he's definitely going to ask."

"What does he think is the reason? Oh no, you said he wouldn't gossip about–"

"I kind of pushed it, well actually I shut him out so he did finally give me his opinion which is that he suspected Arnie had confessed to an affair and wanted forgiveness and reconciliation."

"Then let's go with that. Arnie broke my heart – that much is true – and I don't think I can go back to him. The last bit's a fib, because I already know I can't, but we could say I'll still undecided. I truly am undecided about what I should do."

"You know what you should do, Lila."

"Knowing and being able to act on that knowledge well... be glad you're not in my shoes."

"Those high-heels you wear? I'm *always* glad not to be in them!"

It isn't much of a joke but it helps a little and Lila smiles.

"You know, I do have the option of doing nothing at all. Other than file for divorce, that is. I could just pretend Arnie never told me the truth. It happened 2,000 miles away and I don't ever have to see him again. I can just forget all about it."

Judith studies her friend's face for a long moment before replying:

"No, I really don't think you can."

"I can try."

"You have been trying. Ever since Rev Robbie was killed and you realized he wouldn't be able to counsel you."

"What?"

"Oh Lila, your face when you discovered his body. I've never seen such a look of bleak anguish."

"You're smart, Judith. And you're right, I knew he would steer me in the right direction and insist I follow through. And I'd have to pay attention to him because he is, was, a man of God. He could be very forthright and forceful too when dealing with people being wishy-washy about sin."

"Sin? You didn't commit the crime."

"No, but I'm sure Rev Robbie would tell me that my inaction, my silence, is putting Arnie's immortal soul in jeopardy."

"Oh. Do you believe in that?"

"I'm trying very hard not to."

Chapter Twenty

"I'm glad we've got a chance to get together. I missed you yesterday," says Grant.

"I missed you, too. This is the first Valentine's Day when I've actually been seeing someone and... well, I guess, after all, it really is just another day."

"No, it isn't. It's a day when the someone who's being seen gets to do this..." and with that Grant pulls Judith close and gives her a long, expressive kiss. The fingers of one hand tangle themselves in her hair and he holds the other hand flat along her jaw, keeping her mouth in place. When he pulls back her eyes are still closed and she opens them to see his happy smile. Time suspends for a moment and then Judith gives a little laugh saying:

"Definitely *not* just another day then," and shifts back in her seat widening the space between them. Grant takes the hint.

"So, I've been wanting to hear all about your session with Lila yesterday. What happened with Arnie, and what's going to happen with the two of them?"

"Oh. Oh, it's a bit of a mess actually... nothing's been decided one way or the other. Lila is still trying to sort out her thoughts about it all. Grant, she did ask me not to talk to you about this. I'm sorry, I'm really caught in the middle between you and her."

Judith looks so uncomfortable Grant quickly assures her that he doesn't mean to put her on the spot.

"Don't worry about me, I don't need to know. I'm a nosy guy, probably why I became a detective! but not everything is my business and I'm absolutely fine with that. You can tell Lila with a clear conscience that you didn't tell me a thing, and that I didn't press you."

"Thank you, thank you so much," replies Judith with relief.

"Don't thank me yet because there is a corollary: if I see you looking utterly miserable and burdened by a secret then I will start asking questions and probing but I won't pester you, I'll go straight to Lila."

"That's okay then because I won't let Lila's problems drag me down. I will do my best to help her however I can, but ultimately she'll make her own decision because she's the one who has to live with it."

"Good girl," Grant smiles, and looks ready to draw Judith close again but he sits back instead.

"I spoke with one of the Constables who attended to the crime scene at the school," he began but Judith interrupted to ask,

"The cheeky one?"

"Umm, what do you mean?"

"One of them made it clear that they were dispatched pronto because of my *friendship* with you."

"Oh, he did, did he? Which one?"

"I didn't get a name, but Grant I wouldn't want to get anyone in trouble. I wasn't offended and I was pleased that they showed up so quickly to look after the paperwork so I can send it off to the insurance company."

"The body shop should be able to do that for you, where are you taking the car?"

"Oh my agent emailed me the names of three places in Calgary and suggested I pick one of those. Hang on, let me bring up the email so you can have a look and see if you recognize any names."

"It's probably not a good thing if I recognize the names," he chuckles. Taking her phone he reads the short list and says: "This first place is good. I had work done there a few years back and they've been around a long time. Good reputation."

"Thanks, I'll get in touch with them."

"So anyhow, it looks like there was some degree of planning in this robbery because number one: the thief picked a time when there was nobody outside. A school often has people, students, out and about. And two: there was no rock or anything left at the scene so the perp brought a tool or picked up something to use and then took it away with them. Finally, number three: they didn't rifle through the front-seat console or your glove-box. By the way the Constable told me you don't keep that locked?"

"My glove-box? No, of course not. There's nothing of value."

"Some people keep their GPS device or a battery pack or even cash in their glove-box."

"But I don't so if anyone ever broke in to steal I'd rather they popped it open and saw there was nothing then broke it to bits just to make the same discovery."

Grant thinks about that for a moment before saying,

"Okay, fair point."

"So my car was smashed for the sole purpose of getting at Rev Robbie's books from The Centre."

"Yeah, and since they took his computer too we have no way of–"

"Really? The Centre doesn't have everything backed up to the Cloud? Wow, I would never have guessed they'd be so lax... good thing I have a copy of his computer files."

"What?"

"On my last, no second-last, meeting with him I copied everything over onto a thumb drive. I told him I'd take the physical copies as well in case I needed to find an actual receipt but it wasn't likely. The ledgers and boxes weren't important at all – well, they were but they aren't essential."

"So whatever the thief stole thinking they were covering up... you already have it."

"Yes, I've copied the files onto my laptop so you can take the original thumb drive."

"Judith! this is wonderful news, you're a marvel!"

"Well thank you, but hold the compliments because I've had a quick look over the files and I can't see anything incriminating."

"Ahhh, but you're not a forensic auditor. If there are any secrets they'll be revealed and at least now, thanks to you, we've got some material to work with."

Judith flushes becomingly at Grant's praise and on impulse he leans over and kisses her lips. Startled, but pleased, she looks up with a smile and when their eyes met they each feel the thrill of a momentary connection. This time she doesn't move away but he does, he stands holding up the thumb drive and explains he wants to hand in the evidence right away.

"Can I take you out for dinner this evening?" he asks.

"Oh I think everywhere will be booked, don't you? All the people who didn't manage something yesterday will be celebrating today."

"Well I could get take-out and bring dinner over if..." he leaves the decision with her. Judith holds his gaze while answering:

"That would be lovely, Grant."

He grins happily adding:

"Are we going to keep kissing? because if so, I'd better choose something with no garlic."

"I'll leave that choice up to you," she replies enigmatically.

Chapter Twenty-One

Sunday, February 16, 2020

Judith was enjoying a leisurely, but solitary, breakfast thinking happy thoughts about the night before.

Grant had returned with two dinners from Swiss Chalet that they followed up with the upside-down cake Judith made that afternoon.

"I meant to serve it with whipped cream but I forgot to buy some, sorry!"

"Don't be, this is perfect as is. Such a moist, flavourful cake."

"That's the peaches. I love gingerbread either way: plain or with the added fruit."

"Me too, it's delicious. Thank you for making it for me."

"You're very welcome."

"Do I get to take the rest home?"

"Of course, I'll put it in a tupperware for you."

"Well, not yet, we might eat some more after..." When she lifted an eyebrow he amended that to: "I mean, later. Later with coffee or tea."

Judith hid a smile and handed him the Valentine's Day card she'd bought. He opened it and chuckled at the joke.

"I actually wanted something that said more but the cards at the store all said too much! so in this case I had to settle for *less is more*."

Judith hides a smile and hands him the Valentine's Day card she'd bought. He open it and chuckles at the joke.

"I actually wanted something that said more but the cards at the store all said too much! so in this case I had to settle for less is more."

"It's perfect, thank you again." Grant leans in for a kiss and Judith doesn't pull away so he kisses her again, more deeply. Then he gets up and going to his coat takes out a little wrapped package from the pocket. It is a small box and he hands it to her saying:

"Don't worry, it's not a ring even if the box is that kind of shape!"

Judith makes a production of wiping her forehead with a loud *phew*!

Then she unwraps her gift and finds herself looking at a beautiful pair of emerald stud earrings. They are in a yellow-gold setting with a surround of tiny diamond chips. They are breathtaking, and Judith gives him a wide-eyed, dazzled look.

"They're beautiful, so utterly beautiful!" she exclaims.

"I hoped you'd like them."

"Like them? I LOVE them!" Judith flings her arms around Grant's neck and meets his lips in a warm, passionate kiss. When they break apart she studies the earrings again, saying:

"These are gorgeous. Absolutely perfect! Thank you so so so much! Oh, but they must have cost an awful lot of money?"

"I delighted to spend my money on you, Judith. I noticed that you wear a lot of green so I thought these would match."

"That's so thoughtful! Oh Grant..."

This time when they kiss they don't break apart but lie back against the couch cushions with their arms around each other. Kissing, staring into each other's eyes, then kissing some more. Judith has never been with a man but she trusts Grant and follows his lead.

They end up lying together on the couch and after they've been kissing and exploring with roving hands for some time Grant sits up saying:

"Enough of that missy, you're getting me all worked up. We have a murder to solve so why don't you make me some of your delicious coffee and we'll get cracking. Right after you direct me to your bathroom," he says, standing up.

"Grant there are only four rooms here, how hard can it be to find the toilet? especially for a detective?"

He turns back to look at her saying:

"I don't want to take a wrong turn and end up in your bedroom, Judith."

Part of her wants to ask if it really would be a wrong turn but since that is way too forward she ignores his remark altogether and tells him the bathroom is on the left side.

She makes coffee, cuts Grant another slice of cake, then wraps up the rest for him to take home. She's put in her new earrings and is admiring herself in the mirror at the front door when he comes up behind her. He slides his arms around her waist and she leans against him while they both study the effect. Judith tilt her head and the earrings sparkle in the reflected light.

"I just love them," she says.

With a squeeze he replies: "I'm so glad."

Judith has laid out the coffee and cake in the kitchen's dining area so they sit down there and discuss the murder case.

"Another avenue of investigation led me to the trailer park."

"Ooh, talking like this makes me feel like I'm in an episode of PBS 'Mystery' or something. So exciting!"

"Well, as I mentioned before I need a sounding-board and you're a very good listener, Judith. And you don't interrupt *too* often," replies Grant with a smile.

Judith makes a gesture of zipping her lips shut. Once again she realizes that Grant is a natural-born storyteller, relating the details of his interviews so clearly she feels like she is actually there. She doesn't want to miss a word. He leans forward and using his hands to draw pictures in the air he is able to make his characters live.

"Edgemont Trailer Park has been around for years. These parks get a bad reputation – sometimes deserved – but the Edgemont park is well-run and the residents are law-abiding householders who maintain their properties. However, there are one or two troublemakers.

In this instance the homeowner, a Mr. Jonathan Pederson, an elderly man who lived in the park for many years, was sent to hospital by his home help and subsequently transferred to the hospice. He isn't going to be coming home.

His granddaughter has moved into the trailer and because Mr. Pederson isn't dead there's no will or probate or anything else to stop her from doing so. She is, frankly, an *unsavoury character* and her boyfriend is worse. They're both known to police, and he has a lengthy record.

So Belle Pederson and Antwon Pruitt, which he spells *w-o-n* instead of *o-i-n-e,* are shacked up in the trailer park and causing trouble.

Now the trailer park manager... uh, I should explain. The Edgemont Trailer Park is co-operative housing meaning the land is owned by Edgemont which also pays for a full-time resident manager but the residents own their own trailers and also shares in the co-op itself. They pay a monthly maintenance fee and have a say in how the place is run.

Jerry Bennett, the manager, is really on the ball. He keeps a close eye on the comings and goings of the residents. Quite a few are elderly now and they like having Jerry drop by to check up on them. Belle and Antwon don't like Jerry coming around at all. They had a few run-ins and finally he came to the police station to make a complaint because he said the problem – drugs – was more than he could handle on his own.

We were all a bit surprised about that because the police don't have trouble at the trailer park and that's all down to Jerry. He's always managed to keep things under control without involving us. But drugs... well, that's a different story.

In fact, your old friend Billy MacNeill was mentioned as one of the *bad influences*, as Jerry calls them, hanging around.

Well, as you'll recall we arrested Billy awhile back but I guess he's out on bail.

Anyhow Jerry – he's a big guy, by the way: stands about 6 foot 3 or 4, just over 200 pounds, huge walrus moustache that's still mostly black although his hair has gone gray. Jerry looks to be a match for anyone even though he's gotta be getting up there in years.

So, he comes to the police station to make a report claiming the trouble is coming from the Jonathan Pederson trailer. He explains that the old man is in hospital, well in the Sally Ann, you know, the Salvation Army hospice? and is there anything the police can do to protect his property for him? saying the granddaughter has moved in and brought a noisy, disreputable crowd who, he suspects, are dealing drugs from that location.

It's a tricky situation though, because the girl claims she has permission from her grandpa to live there but he's not well enough to tell us if that's true. If she's lying we could charge her with trespassing but we can't prove she's lying.

So all they do at the station is tell Jerry Bennett to get the trailer park co-op to find out who Mr. Pederson's lawyer is, and see if they have a will or any written instructions from him. The girl definitely is his granddaughter, but if she isn't his heir then whoever is supposed to inherit can hire a lawyer and issue an eviction notice. But none of that addresses the immediate issue of Jerry's suspicions that drugs are being dealt out of that trailer.

As you know, though, someone's suspicions aren't enough for us to act on. A patrolman went by to knock on the door but Belle Pederson wouldn't let him in and it's her right not to do so. The officer had nothing to report that we could use. For example, if he believed someone was in imminent danger – like a screaming child – then he could have entered the premises without a warrant but that wasn't the case.

So, Jerry came away frustrated with us and our inability to do anything. Since then he's taken to sitting in the common area with a few like-minded residents who are taking photos of everyone coming and going along with pictures of the licence plates on their cars. I don't know if that's going to rattle anybody enough to slow down business but it might, however it's a bit of a risky manoeuvre, from our point of view.

So that's the unsatisfactory situation at the trailer park. Now, *the plot thickens* because we learned that Rev Robbie was out there at the trailer park a couple of days before he was killed. Trouble is, we don't know if he went there to remonstrate with the alleged dealers – apparently there have been stories of drugs coming into The Centre – or if he went there as a customer to buy."

"Surely not," interrupts Judith.

"That's my thinking too but then how did Rev Robbie die from an overdose of the latest popular drug: Fentanyl?"

Grant left shortly after their conversation taking the other half of his cake with him.

Judith has a busy Sunday, much better than the previous week, taking care of household chores like grocery shopping, housework, and laundry, but all the while last night's conversation is playing in her mind.

After dinner she calls Grant and is pleased to get hold of him on the first try. She's been giving their discussion about the drugs a lot of thought and a nagging idea just won't leave her.

After the preliminary greetings and the endearments that naturally come about after their closeness last night Judith tells him she's had a thought she needs to share.

"First off, did you ever meet Rev Robbie?"

"I did, but we were in a crowd, I never got a chance to speak to the man one-to-one. But from everything I've heard about him I'm sure I would have liked and respected him."

"Oh, for sure you would have. He always spoke quietly, like never raising his voice or shouting, but he was forceful in making his point. There was no pretending innocence or lack of understanding with Rev

Robbie! Even Lila mentioned he could zero in on sin and be relentless in pushing you do the right thing. And that's the point:

I think Rev Robbie caught someone with drugs at The Centre and–"

"But surely he would have turned them in," interrupts Grant.

"No, hear me out. I think he caught someone with just enough for their own use, not dealing, and he confiscated the drugs. That means he had to take them from someone who couldn't intimidate him. So not a drug dealer, not a gang member, not one of the guys you described from the trailer park. No, I think it was a young person. So say Rev Robbie takes away the drugs well he wouldn't just stick them in his pocket or toss them in a drawer, he'd lock them away to keep everyone safe."

"He'd put them in the safe."

"Yes! and, if he believed it was a first-time offence and that the young person, 'cause it could be a boy or a girl, if he thought that putting them through the justice system really wouldn't be justice – and you can be sure he had his own high standards there – then I don't think he'd call the police. I think he'd try to handle the situation himself."

Slowly Grant completes the thought: "And that decision forced the killer's hand."

"Exactly. The killer – or killers, I guess I should say – didn't exactly panic because there was some planning involved but they must have acted quickly. So, what young people were around that day or at the most the day before? and who else might have known about the drugs in the safe? Who was around who knew the combination to the safe? or which of Rev Robbie's visitors that day was comfortable enough with for him to open the safe himself while they were there? There might be other questions but those ones have been nagging at me. So far, the only answer I can come up with is the volleyball team."

"The whole team?"

"No, don't joke it isn't funny."

"I know, I'm sorry. It's just I started this phone-call with no suspects and all of a sudden I have six – it is six players on a volleyball team, right?"

"Maybe seven or eight with substitutes. No actually there would be more because it's a tournament so more than one team would have been in The Centre practising."

"Oh cool even more suspects! Well thanks for that, Judith!"

"So do you think the killer intended to kill? Maybe they just wanted to incapacitate Rev Robbie long enough for them to get their drugs back?"

"Or maybe they wanted to get him high and incoherent so he'd lose credibility. Any accusations he might make wouldn't carry much weight if he himself was a suspected drug user. There were only very faint traces of Fentanyl left behind in the safe but enough to identify the drug."

"Lots to think about."

"I do thank you for your help, it really is a help you know."

"Good night, Grant."

"What do you think about me coming over so we can brainstorm some more?" he asks hopefully.

"Good night, Grant," Judith repeats, but with a smile sounding in her voice.

"You don't have to work tomorrow, right? It's Family Day—"

"Good night, Grant," she interrupts, adding: "I'll dream about you." Then disconnects while chuckling at his groan.

Chapter Twenty-Two

Monday, February 17, 2020

Judith waits until 10:00 before phoning Lila but even so her friend's voice sounds sleepy.

"Sorry, did I wake you?"

"I was dozing, I haven't been sleeping too well."

"I'm not surprised but listen – today's a holiday so what do you think about spending the day together, just the two of us, and I promise not to say a word about the Arnie thing although of course I'm willing to listen if you want to talk. But if not we'll have a holiday from our problems, okay?"

"Oh that sounds very okay. What do you feel like doing? Have you been bitten by the gambling bug and want to go back to the casino?"

"No way, I want to do something outdoors. Would you be interested in going to the Zoo? Even at this time of year there's plenty to see."

"I'd love to! I love zoos and I haven't been to the Calgary Zoo yet."

"Oh you're in for a treat. I go there so often I've got a pass for admission and parking! and I get a discounted friend rate so today will be my treat and it will cost me practically nothing."

"You accountant-types... I need a coffee and a shower but I can be ready right after. Do you want me to pick you up?"

"No, I'll have to drive because my free parking is based on my licence plate. How about if I'm at your door in say... 45 minutes?"

"Perfect, and Judith? thanks for this. I really appreciate it."

"That's what friends are for!"

* * * * * *

Warmly dressed with scarves, mitts, and hats the two women have a great day out. Lila says the Calgary Zoo compares very favourably to the Toronto Zoo, adding that it's so well laid out. She likes the fact that they see plenty of animals who have room to roam without lots and lots of walking from one exhibit to the next.

Despite it being February they each have an ice-cream and decide they don't want a big dinner, settling on a fish and chip supper that Lila pays for. Since they can see the coffee looking black sitting in its half-full pot they decide to wait until they can stop at a Tim Horton's. They find one on the way back to Lila's and have their hot drinks in the car in the parking lot. That's when Judith speaks seriously about her relationship with Grant and the next step.

"I know he wants to make love to me but I also know that he isn't in love with me."

"Okay, how do you know that?"

"Well, he wanted to come over quite late last night so—"

"That's not what I meant," laughs Lila. "He's probably wanted to have sex with you since the first time you two met. That's how guys are, they look at every woman with sex on their brain."

"Ewww, no way."

"Yeah, Arnie told me that years ago. We were arguing about some guy and I was saying *he's just a friend* and Arnie's like *there's no such thing* and he's wrong about that, but he might be right about what the guys are thinking even if they really do just want to be friends. Arnie said guys think that way even about women they don't want to screw. I have no reason to doubt him, I mean it's not the kind thing you'd brag about is it?"

"You know you're guilty of that yourself, aren't you?"

"What?!"

"For awhile there it seemed like you were trying to match me with every guy we met, remember?"

"Well, we were suddenly seeing a lot of three really handsome men: Brian Penner, Noel Larkin, and George Grant – your Grant. All are total hunks."

"Besides being engaged already Noel is too young for us, and I see you put Brian at the top of the list..."

"Yeah well I wasn't thinking marriage. Judith! are you still a virgin waiting for your wedding night?"

"Yes, and no–"

Lila laughs again saying: "Sorry, but that actually is a *yes or no* question!"

"Yes, I'm a virgin but no, I'm not particularly waiting for marriage... I've just never had a boyfriend."

"Are you serious? Judith, you don't have a pretty face exactly but you're still really good looking, and as I've mentioned before, you've got a great body. I can't believe guys haven't chased after you."

"Oh, I've had offers – propositions, actually – but from married men. Even when I was in school the guys who came on to me were already living with, or married to, someone else. It really turned me off. I mean, why bother to get involved with someone if you're only going to cheat on them? That makes no sense. So no, no boyfriends."

"So then how can you know that Grant isn't *in* love with you?"

"Well, why would he be? I mean, he's really only known me for a few months and we didn't start dating right away. No, we'll have to get to know each other a lot better before we can fall in love."

"You don't believe in love at first sight?"

"Oh! well, attraction and, um, lust at first sight, sure. But no, not real love."

"Real love as opposed to lust love?"

"Ummm, something like that."

"So you're not in love with Grant because you haven't known him long enough *to* fall in love, is that right?"

"Uhhh, yeah... yeah, that's right."

"So you don't love Grant."

"Oh, no."

"But you're thinking of sleeping with him? Judith, you slut!"

"LILA! stop laughing at me!"

"I can't! you're too funny, Judith. Listen, it sounds like you're ready, so I guess just let Nature take its course. It'll happen when it happens... but make sure you shave your legs and pits every day and wear matching bra and panties."

"I always do."

"Yeah, that figures. And hey, you have to promise that after it happens you'll tell me right away!"

"God, we sound like teenagers."

"Oh Judith, most teenage girls have already done it!"

Judith doesn't speak to Grant that day. She'd sent him a text in the morning explaining she and Lila were spending the holiday at the Zoo and he'd answered *have fun*. Just before she gets into her bed that night a second text arrives saying he hopes she and Lila had a good day, and he's looking forward to seeing her soon.

She replies "me 2 xxx".

Chapter Twenty-Three

Tuesday, February 18, 2020

A light tap-tap on the door frame signals Beth Penner's arrival at Judith's office in the school library. The girl's looks and manner have changed over the last while. Beth is still a quiet, unassuming girl but she is far less hesitant and shy. The events of the last couple of months brought added maturity to the girl who was already quite self-contained, and of course, she's at the age of physical growth spurts, too.

Judith closes the file on her laptop and clicks off the screen while motioning the girl to come in and sit down.

"Hello Beth, you're looking well. That's a great colour on you – it really brings out your eyes."

The girl gives a close-mouthed smile that dimples her blushing cheeks. Beth is turning into a very pretty teenager, especially since she hasn't coated her eyelashes in thick black mascara or chosen unsuitable lipstick.

Edgemont School for Girls is strict about not allowing excessive make-up on the students, with Principal Johnson as the sole arbiter of what constitutes *excessive*. Some of the girls try to get around the stricture by having their make-up tattooed on, or semi-permanently applied, but in those instances the Principal calls the parent for a chat and when the time comes for a touch-up that work isn't performed.

However the school has no rules regarding the students' hair styles or lengths or colours – only that it has to be clean. Pat confided to Judith that she has to let the girls enjoy some freedom of expression and whereas skillfully applied make-up could add years to a teenager's face, a messy punky hairdo won't do so.

"Sorry to bother you when you're busy Ms. Taylor but I'm a bit concerned, mostly about Margaret Seely, but also about Ms. Morelli, and I hoped I could have a word." Beth's anxiety shows up in the way she is rubbing her fingers tightly together.

At least she's not biting her nails or cuticles, thinks Judith before saying: "Absolutely, what's on your mind?"

Beth inhales a deep breath and explains: "I've been seeing quite a bit of Margaret lately because her mother is never home so she's been coming over to our house a lot. Lila – she said it's okay to call her Lila when we're not at school – would stop by quite often too, and we'd play board games or cards or watch a movie on TV. Sometimes Dad orders in a pizza or chicken and he always takes us out for Taco Tuesdays. If something comes up and he has to work then Lila treats us. We've all gotten used to it but Ms. Morelli doesn't come by any more, not even on Tuesdays, and Margaret is... well, she's angry all the time."

Judith considers about how much she can say and decides to be as upfront as possible with Beth. She knows Beth's attachment to Lila runs deep so the girl must be hurting at being shut out. *I know that feeling!* thinks Judith.

"Beth, this is confidential but of course you can share it with your father, just like you can always repeat to him anything an adult tells you, even if they say it's a secret, right?" The girl nods in agreement. "Okay then, I'm relying on your discretion and your friendship with Lila.

I don't know if you realize that Lila is actually a married woman? She is estranged from her husband who lives in Toronto."

The girl nods more vigorously so Judith pauses to let her explain.

"Lila told us. I think Dad was going to ask her out on a date – you know, just the two of them – but maybe she thought so too because right out of the blue she told us she was married but she and her husband were living apart. Far apart, he lives in Ontario!

She's booked a flight back to Toronto on April 9th in order to spend Easter with her parents and, she said, *to come to terms with her marriage*. She also said she's pretty sure it's over but she wants to be certain. Because the next day is Good Friday she'll get an extra-long weekend and she said that will be enough time for her trip."

"Oh, I didn't realize she as going away for Easter. You see Lila and I had grown quite close but something happened at the beginning of January and since then Lila has been withdrawn. It sounds like she's been distancing herself from you and your father as well.

What happened is that her husband flew out here to visit. Lila was looking forward to seeing him but I'm pretty sure things didn't go well. I don't know why, because she won't say, however she will talk things over with me, and with you two as well, I'm sure, once she gets it all sorted out in her own mind first."

Beth sighs deeply saying: "I... I guess I should be sorry if her marriage is in trouble but I'm not. I don't want her to move back to Toronto, I want her to stay here and go on dates with my Dad. But, that's being selfish."

"Then that makes me selfish too because it's what I'd like as well." Judith replies with a smile. They sit silently for a moment sharing their mutual interest. Finally Judith says:

"Now, what's all this about Margaret Seely? What is she so angry about?"

"Her mother, I guess. Mrs. Seely is hardly ever home and even when she is she doesn't seem to have any time for Margaret. Instead she's on her computer all the time and then, when Margaret's in bed, she sometimes hears her mother taking the car out. Late at night."

"And leaving Margaret alone in the house?"

"Yes but... I'm pretty sure Margaret wouldn't want me to tell anyone about that, she's only ten or soon to be ten and afraid of being taken away–"

"She doesn't have to worry about that, it's not illegal to leave a child that age alone here in Alberta. It's up to the parent's to decide what's best, but if there are issues Child Protective Services can step in. Like, if she was being left for long periods of time or if there was something harmful in the house like a handgun."

"Oh no, I don't think there's anything like that. My Dad has some hunting rifles but he keeps them in a gun safe and has his certificate and licence and everything. No, Margaret is just worried about whatever it is her mother is doing because it seems like it's a big secret."

"Where is Margaret's father? Do you know?"

"Oh yeah, she talks about him a lot. Her mother kicked him out, but he was always away a lot anyways because he travels so much for his business. That's what Margaret told us. Now when he comes to Calgary he stays at the Palliser which is really nice, and Margaret gets to stay overnight with him. It has a swimming pool plus sometimes they go to the zoo and have brunch there. She really misses her Dad."

"That's a shame. Maybe Mr. and Mrs. Seely will be able to work things out?"

"From what people are saying it doesn't sound like she wants Mr. Seely back."

"What do you mean?"

"Well..." the girl is obviously embarrassed so Judith figured she'd heard some of the stories circulating about Andrea Seely and that young man, Kyle Danby.

"Never mind, Beth. We can't solve the Seely's problems, but I hope I've given you some insight into what's going on with Lila right now. She needs us to give her space and time and that's what we have to do."

"Yes, I'll tell Dad what you told me because he was wondering if he'd scared her away but he didn't, did he?"

"No, you can reassure your father on that point."

The girl bounces out of her chair like she didn't have a care in the world. The *resiliency of youth*, Judith thinks to herself.

She wonders if she should have a word with Pat Johnson about Margaret Seely's home situation? but decides not to. While Judith can hear a rumour and call it hearsay the school principal has to act on any supposition if one of her student's is possibly in harm's way.

She decides she'll give the situation some more thought, but unfortunately circumstances dictate otherwise.

Chapter Twenty-Four

Tuesday, February 18, 2020

The sight of Margaret Seely slumped on the bench outside Principal Johnson's office with her arms tightly crossed, her heels drumming, and her face red with fury is almost enough to make Judith turn around. But when Pat called her she agreed to help so she can't turn back now. She sits down beside the girl and asks:

"What's going on, Margaret?"

The girl tucks her chin into her chest and commences rocking back and forth but doesn't say a word.

"You're obviously angry about something, so please tell me what it is."

Still no eye contact or verbal response from Margaret. Changing tactics – and resisting a strong urge to shake the girl – Judith deliberately softens her tone and asks in a syrupy voice:

"Do you need to have a good cry? Hmm? Is that it?"

And a small tornado erupts with Margaret on her feet stomping up and down while loudly shouting that she never never never ever cries. Principal Johnson opens her office door and commands silence:

"Stop that racket right now, Margaret Seely. You're already in more than enough trouble, you don't need to be adding to it. Get in here and sit down quietly."

Judith finds herself actually feeling a bit sorry for Margaret when she sees how the girl deflates under the voice of authority. With her head bowed and shoulders drooping Margaret slowly shuffles into the office and sits in the furthest chair.

"Since we're unable to reach either of your parents, Margaret, I've asked Ms. Taylor to sit in as your Appropriate Adult. Due to the seriousness of the situation, and the school's policy of zero tolerance for fighting, we need to deal with this right away.

Let's begin."

Pat thanks Judith for taking on the supportive *in loco parentis* role. She introduces the other woman in the room, a Mrs. Vivian Sanderson, who Judith has previously met in her job as the school's bursar.

Vivian, a good-looking woman dressed in soccer mom gear, is accompanied by her daughter April who has obviously been crying and now sports a bruised and swollen lip.

Margaret Seely sits quietly but directs a poisonous glare at the older girl.

"April, please tell us what happened outside at lunchtime."

The girl sniffs loudly before turning to meet Margaret's eyes and pointing at her says:

"SHE punched me. She busted my lip and made it bleed. She's violent and mean."

Before Margaret can respond Principal Johnson holds up her hand palm out saying:

"You will get your chance, Margaret. For now it's April's turn to speak." Then turning to April and her mother she asks: "Why did Margaret punch you?"

"Because she's crazy," spit April, just as her mother is saying:

"Surely the 'why' doesn't matter when the result is a physical injury like this. Look at my daughter's mouth! There's no disputing what happened."

"And I'm not disputing it, Ms. Sanderson. I've already spoken to other witnesses who confirm that Margaret Seely knocked April to the ground and punched her, hard, in the mouth. It's a very serious offence with consequences which is why it's vital to get all the facts on the record."

"Now, April. Please answer the question properly. What did you do, or say, to provoke Margaret's actions?"

Again Vivian Sanderson expostulates angrily claiming Principal Johnson is blaming the victim.

"It doesn't matter what happened before the physical assault because there is no justification for it, none, no matter what was said."

Pat Johnson waits a moment in silence, allowing the upset mother to regain her composure.

"I agree, Ms. Sanderson. There is no justification for violence however, something provoked nine-year-old Margaret into launching an attack against thirteen-year-old April. I want to know what that something was."

"I'm almost ten," states Margaret. We all look at her and notice she is a rather puny-sized girl compared to the tall and stoutly built April.

"Did you push Margaret or hit her first?"

"No! of course not. Nobody can say I did 'cause I didn't touch her."

"Then what was it you said to upset her so much?"

Caught out April folds her lips together as well as she can with the swelling, and wears a stubborn expression on her face.

"I can't make you give your side of the story if you don't want to, April, but a victim's statement does impact the offender's punishment."

"Oh just spit it out April, I don't want to spend all day here."

"Welllll, I might have said some something about how everybody's laughing about her mother being a real cougar always chasing after that Kyle Danby."

Vivian Sanderson briefly closes her eyes but my gaze turns to Margaret to see hers filling up with tears.

"It's not true, take it back! my mother isn't doing anything like that. You're calling her names, calling her catty and she's not!"

I look at Pat and see she realizes, as I do, that Margaret doesn't understand the insulting 'cougar' reference. Glancing over at Vivian her exasperated expression tells me she's picked up on that as well.

"April, why are you repeating gossip? You don't even know what you're saying."

"Mom, it's not me it's everybody. They're all saying it."

"Well, I'm ashamed of you for joining in. Of course that's still no excuse for the fight," she finishes, turning back to Pat.

"No, you're right. There is no excuse."

"So what happens now?"

"I will consider everything I've heard and determine Margaret's punishment."

"The school's policy on fighting is suspension—" Vivian begins but Pat interrupts her saying coolly:

"I'm well aware of the policy, after all I'm the one who wrote it, so yes, Margaret will definitely be suspended. The question I have to consider is – for how long?"

"Well, what's the normal time?"

"Actually fighting isn't normal at Edgemont School for Girls so there's no precedent for me to follow," Pat pauses again, quite effectively, to let that statement sink in.

"I do feel that Margaret coming to the defence of her mother's reputation deserves more leniency then if she'd struck out because of name-calling against herself. And, of course, April should definitely have know better than to hurt the feelings of a much younger girl by spreading a rumour."

Everyone sits in silent expectation but Pat merely reverts to formal Principal mode and thanks Vivian Sanders for coming in before escorting her to the door suggesting April might like to leave school early today.

"But I've got Art Class this afternoon," whines the girl and her mother says she can stay if she likes. The two of them leave and Judith signals to Pat with her eyes asking whether or not she should follow. She indicates yes, but not until instructing Margaret to thank Ms. Taylor for interrupting her work on Margaret's behalf.

Margaret, still determined not to make eye contact with adults, mumbles a 'thank you and sorry, Ms. Taylor' which Judith graciously accepts while winking at Pat.

As she leaves the room she can hear the girl telling the principal she'd much rather have had Ms. Lila because she, at least, would have stuck up for her.

Chapter Twenty-Five

Wednesday, February 19, 2020

"Judith? It's Samira. Can you come down to the principal's office? the sooner the better."

"Sure, but why didn't Pat call me directly? is she okay?"

"Yes, but she's on a conference call with some trustees, I'm afraid Andrea Seely is stirring up trouble. I think Pat needs your moral support."

"I'm on my way,"

Judith hangs up and thinks for a moment. Pat in a tizzy is not a pretty sight but Pat in a white-hot rage well, that most certainly is something best avoided. She'll have to do her best to calm her boss down.

After yesterday's lunchtime meeting about the schoolgirls fighting Judith has typed up notes of the conversation on her computer. She prints the sheet off now and takes it with her. Arriving at the principal's office she waits outside with Samira until Pat's call ends.

Both women enter the inner office. Pat waves them to chairs then dry-washes her face with her strong, capable hands. Judith is just thinking *it's a good thing Pat doesn't wear make-up* when Samira suggests:

"Pat, put on some lipstick, it will make you feel better."

"You mean like war paint?"

Samira shrugs, "Call it what you like, to me it's like armour so yeah, I guess war paint is appropriate."

"I've got Andrea Seely coming in and she's bringing Margaret because she thinks Margaret is starting back in class today. She isn't. I gave her a three-day suspension and she won't be welcome back until Monday."

"So am I here to referee or what?"

"Ha, maybe! No, you are my witness. I told Ms. Seely she's welcome to bring along her own."

"Hmm, frankly I'd be surprised if she has a lot of friends."

Just then we hear Andrea Seely arrive with Margaret in tow.

"Run along to your class now, Margaret," she commands but Principal Johnson overrules her telling Margaret to sit quietly in the secretary's office with Samira. As Ms. Seely opens her mouth to protest Pat gestures her into the big office. The strong smell of her too-liberally applied perfume quickly fills the room.

"You know Judith Taylor, our bursar. Ms. Taylor is here as witness in case a third party account of our interaction is required. Please be seated."

Pat takes her chair and switches on the tape recorder she keeps on her desk announcing into it the date, the names of those present, and a statement that this meeting has been requested by Ms. Andrea Seely, parent to student Margaret Seely.

"Go ahead, Ms. Seely."

"Fine. My name is Andrea Seely, I am Margaret's mother therefore a school parent, parent of a paying student, and also a Board Member and Treasurer of The Centre.

My daughter has been suspended from school on the ridiculous charge of fighting with another student. That's simply not possible. Also, it's inconvenient. I have many committments on my time and I can't have my child sent home on a whim. She needs the structure and supervision of school. Margaret must be accepted back into her classes immediately."

"Ms. Seely, Edgemont School for Girls has a strict code of conduct. That's one of the reasons why you have put your daughter in our care. I'm sure you will agree that it would be remiss of me not to impose the standard punishments when required.

Our disciplinary policy for fist-fighting is mandatory suspension. The number of days are at my discretion, probably one to two weeks would be usual, but there is no precedent because in all the years that I have been principal here I have never had to deal with this offence. However, Margaret is an exceptional student with an excellent record for good conduct so I'm being lenient on her. I sent her home for these three days: Wednesday, Thursday, and Friday and I do not expect to see her back here until Monday."

"But you can't suspend Margaret!" cries Andrea Seely.

"I assure I can, and I have done so." Principal Johnson is implacable.

"I can't stay home with her until Monday morning! I have things to do."

"Well, Margaret is not under house arrest, you'll just have to take her with you. You mentioned that you're busy with work for The Centre and I know she'll be welcome there."

"No, I don't want to take her!" Andrea Seely is practically shouting.

There is really nothing to say to an outburst like that. Pat and I simply sit there watching the warring emotions cross the distraught mother's face. She chooses anger, and casting a scathing look at Judith declares:

"I'll be complaining to my School Trustee!" before hurrying out of the room and slamming the door behind her. We could hear her call sharply to Margaret to *come along, NOW!!*

"I don't know why she threatened me, I never said a word," complains Judith.

"That's probably why... she saw you as the weak link."

"Oh thanks Pat. You keep dragging me in here for one Seely thing after another and all I get are insults!"

"You're welcome, Judith," said Pat with a chuckle. "I know you can take it."

Chapter Twenty-Six

Thursday, February 20, 2020

Judith is outside the nurse's office next morning, waiting for Lila. The meeting with Andrea Seely has nagged at her all evening. She's kicking herself for not speaking up. She should have pointed out that Margaret is being left on her own far too much, and the fist-fight is a sign of a deeper problem. The girl is filled with anger and acting out, reacting to her parent's separation, and resenting her mother.

She wants to rant and rave a bit but changes her mind when sees how tired and haggard her friend looks.

"My heart is breaking for you, Lila. You're exhausted. You're under enormous strain and something's got to give. It'll be your sanity if this keeps up."

"Well good morning to you too, Judith."

"Oh stop. You're killing yourself bit by bit, Arnie's secret is eating you up."

"Arnie's secret is off-limits. Talk to me about something else."

"Okay, how about when's the last time you saw Beth Penner or her Dad, or Margaret Seely? They all miss spending time with you. And Margaret – of all people – has taken to fighting in the schoolyard."

"No way!"

"She's currently under suspension."

"Margaret Seely?! she's like what, nine years old?"

"*Almost ten* is how she puts it, and yes, she was fighting. I got called in as the appropriate adult although she made it clear she'd much rather have had you."

"Oh jeez, what's been going on?"

"Just life, Lila. Everybody else is living it but Arnie has taken yours away. You've been in limbo or something for the last six weeks."

"Oh I know, I know. I just can't make up my mind, I can't. I don't know what to do. I'm not a ditherer but all of a sudden I am because it's not my secret. That's the real problem. I can handle my own messes but I don't know what to do with Arnie's."

"Yes you do, Lila. You have to tell Arnie that if he doesn't turn himself in you will. He dumped this on you because he wants *you* to make the decision–"

"No! he swore me to secrecy."

"And he had no right to do so! If he wanted to keep it a secret he should have kept his mouth shut."

"But I pushed and pushed him to tell me what was wrong. I can't complain now that he's done so."

"Of course you can. Look, you pushed because you wanted to help–"

"Yeah well, the road to hell really is paved with good intentions."

"Lila, listen. He needed a push, you gave it, he confessed to you and eased his burden but that's not helping, not in the long run, he needs to face up to what he's done. His delay has already cost him his marriage – what else is going to lose?"

"Rev Robbie would say *his soul.*"

"Rev Robbie would say *Lila I'm going to kick your butt if you don't drag that husband of yours to the police station pronto!*"

"Oh Judith, you're right. He would say that," she gave a sad chuckle, "But I'm not ready yet."

"Yes, you are. You don't need any more time to think about it. You know the difference between right and wrong, you have to help him acknowledge it, too. Please, Lila. If you can't convince Arnie to tell your family then you'll have to do it yourself. And ask them to help him navigate the legal system. Lila, he could have just stayed in Toronto and kept his mouth shut while waiting for you to file divorce papers. He told you for a reason. You have to help him."

"Oh dammit, Judith. Now you've given me even more stuff to think about and my head's already pounding. Look, Arnie's been calling and I told him I'd let him know what I decided before the weekend. Just give me another 24 hours."

"Lila, I wish I could say I'll give you all the time in the world but I know I wouldn't be doing you any favours if I said that. This is just such a horrible, horrible situation and I'm so sorry you're in it."

"Thank you for that, my friend."

"You know, speaking of Rev Robbie just now reminded me that he admonished me in his gentle but persistent way for not having pushed you into confiding your secret. I told him at the time that I respected your privacy but... well, he made me feel like I'd failed you and wasn't a good friend."

"You are, Judith, never doubt it."

Feeling ready to tackle any chore Judith carries on to her office resolved to get in touch with Andrea Seely and speak her mind. Her feistiness has to be contained though because she gets the Seely's answering machine and, worried that Margaret might hear the message, has to be very guarded in what she says.

Chapter Twenty-Seven

The end of the school day can't come soon enough for Judith. She is eager to find out what Lila is going to tell Arnie. Not least because Judith is feeling a bit anxious about keeping the secret from Grant any longer.

Just as Judith is packing up her desk for the weekend Lila appears in her doorway.

"Come on in, I've been wondering what your plans are."

"Well, I'm not giving Arnie an answer right now–"

"But you said you would!" interrupts Judith. "I can't keep this from Grant any longer. He's got to be told."

"Judith! It's really not Grant's business – or yours, for that matter."

"Yes, it is. It became my business when you told me the truth. I know I pestered you to tell me so I've only got myself to blame but there it is. I can't unhear the words. You know what I mean, you probably feel exactly the same way."

"I do, except I needed to know. In the wee hours of the morning, when I was tossing and turning, I had the most awful thought: what if instead of telling me the truth Arnie had made up some plausible story that I believed and we got back together? It would never have felt right because he'd always know he was living with a horrible secret and a lie like that it always going to come out eventually. Thank God he was only evasive and didn't actually lie to me."

"Oh Lila, you really are *between a rock and a hard place*. As for Grant, well I've already held back for a week and he's curious. I feel that if I keep this from him any longer then I will be wronging him."

"I see that, I do, but... here's what I've decided: I had planned on flying to Toronto for Easter with my parents but instead I've bumped up the trip so I can take Arnie to the police. I've let him know I'm coming home tomorrow but I haven't told him my decision yet. I have to do that face-to-face.

I already told him our marriage is over but he probably figures he can change my mind. He can't, and he'll realize that because I'm staying with my parents, not in my own home.

I hate burdening my parents but they hate being left out of the loop even more, so... I will tell them first and then we'll enlist whichever of my relatives will be able to help out the best. I still have no guarantee that Arnie will co-operate, but he'll know that I've revealed his secret and there's no turning back from that."

"Oh Lila. It's hard but, it's the right thing to do and you know that, right?"

Lila studies her friend for a moment before answering in a quiet voice:

"I do, but I also know that I feel betrayed by you, Judith. I feel you've pushed me into this position which, I believe I would have come to eventually because it is the right thing to do, but, as I say I feel you've forced my hand. I'm afraid I find that unforgivable, at least for now, but I hope I'll change my mind."

With that she gets up and leaves. Judith stays behind her desk, stunned and tearful. Lila's calm rejection is devastating.

Judith thinks about how she and Grant had originally been so sure Arnie had confessed to an affair and wanted a second chance and that Lila was dealing with betrayal when in fact the truth is so much worse. Arnie committed a crime. An accident, yes, but his failing to report it was deliberate act, a criminal act.

It occurs to Judith that the idea of Arnie-the-Adulterer serves as a very effective distraction. It's such a *cliche,* making it easy to look down on him. It certainly is a million miles away from Arnie-the-Killer. The killer has been effectively disguised by the sleazy, repentant husband.

What if someone else is playing that same game of misdirection?

She immediately thinks of how everyone is sniggering over Andrea-Seely-the-Cougar, but what if that's merely a cover-up? No one is looking past the shameless behaviour that discredits the woman and makes her ridiculous. No one considers that maybe there is a calculating mind plotting the camouflage to hide Andrea-the-Killer?

Have we all been tricked by the stereotype of a sex-starved woman grasping for a last chance at fulfillment? she wonders.

A sudden cacophony of emergency vehicle sirens: fire, police, ambulance shatters the air. Looking out the window Judith can see a line of flashing red lights heading east where black smoke is just visible as it rapidly billows upwards.

* * * * * *

At least four people died in the fire at the trailer park and two fire-fighters were sent to hospital with serious injuries.

Jerry Bennett, the trailer park manager, has suffered second-degree burns to his face and hands. Half his moustache is burned off. When Grant speaks to the man the skin of his face has already turned red and glossy-looking. He is probably in severe pain but reaction hasn't set in yet. He is still distraught over the lives lost.

The fire's point-of-origin is the Pederson trailer, taken over by the granddaughter and her squatter friends, so that is no surprise. Both the girl and her boyfriend are believed to be among the victims but it is too soon for official identifications. Everyone deplores the loss of young life but no one actually liked Belle Pederson or Antwon Pruitt so their passing isn't mourned.

The group of residents who volunteer to keep an eye on that trailer were quick to call in the emergency response teams but the explosion generated extremely high heat and shooting flames so it was impossible to do more than contain it, and try to protect the trailer homes nearby. During all the excitement, fear, and noise an older resident suffers a heart attack but is expected to recover fully.

Fire trucks respond from all the surrounding communities and the investigating team has come from Calgary. The older fire-fighters recognize the sweet smell and quickly surmise that someone free-basing cocaine is the culprit.

"I haven't heard of that in a long time," comments Grant.

The crew members who are gathered around nod in agreement.

"That's because crack's become so popular. It gives pretty much the same punch as free-base but it's a lot safer. Easier to get hold of, too."

"Yeah, and you don't need ether to make it."

Grant turns to the Fire Chief asking: "Ether? that's used in free-basing?"

"It's the most, or was the most, commonly used solvent to *free* the cocaine from its *base*. Unfortunately for everyone involved it's also highly flammable. Crack just needs baking soda and boiling water."

"And smoking crack is the most addictive form of cocaine use, so that's another reason the dealers prefer it."

The horrible smell from the burning hangs in the air, and the stomach-churning sight of melted household goods haunts the witnesses.

Chapter Twenty-Eight

Saturday, February 22, 2020

Although he'd showered when he got home last night and then again this morning Grant thinks he can still smell the fire like it's embedded in his skin. *Maybe it is in my nostrils, throat, lungs?* he wonders.

When Judith opens the door to Grant she notices he looks sad and exhausted, but he brightens considerably on seeing her welcoming face, saying:

"You are a sight for sore eyes, sweetheart."

Judith bows her head, shy at the compliment but pleased. She has taken extra care getting ready using a new shampoo and conditioner, putting on mascara, and adding a dab of perfume to each of her pulse points. She wants to look and feel her very best since she is hoping for a special night.

He reaches out and lifting her chin meets her lips with a soft kiss, then he pulls her close and just stands there for a long moment hugging her to him.

Judith is happy to provide comfort. She's seen the news coverage of the fire and of course the phone lines have been humming as people pass on what they've heard and guessed at, and wondering if she has anything new to add.

"So, what's happening with Lila? You mentioned she was sorting things out by today – or yesterday, rather."

"Oh I let's not talk about that. Lila doesn't want me to say anything to you anyhow."

Grant found that suspicious and asks: "Why not?"

"Just because... it's a sad and sordid story and with the fire last night you've had your fill of death and destruction–"

"Death? What do you mean?"

"Grant, really, let's just leave it for now. Let's forget about other people's problems and just concentrate on each other, here, together..."

"Judith I would love to, truly truly truly, but I can't ignore it when you mention a death. Who died?"

"A homeless person, a bag-lady, Arnie ran her down–"

"WHAT?" Grant yelps but when Judith tries to continue he holds up his hand to stop her insisting:

"No! Don't tell me another word. Omigod, Judith! You've known about this for like a week?"

She isn't sure if she could speak yet so she just nods.

"How could you do that to me? Do you have any idea how much trouble I would be in for even hearing the little bit you've just said? My whole career – poof, gone – in one minute. Jesus Christ, Judith. I can't believe you'd do that to me–"

"Grant, I haven't done anything to you," Judith cries. "This has nothing to do with you, it all happened back in Toronto so–"

"Nothing to do with me? You're making me an accessory to a felony."

"I'm not! You don't know the story yet–"

He interrupts again: "And we'll keep it that way, right? Don't make things worse, don't say another word about it. Judith, shit, I can't believe you put me in this position."

"But I didn't know, I mean this is Alberta so you can't be responsible for what happens in Ontario!"

"No, but I am guilty if I keep silent. You should know that law enforcement personnel are held to a higher standard of conduct than civilians! I *have* to report the possibility that Arnie Morelli has committed–"

"His name isn't Morelli, that's Lila's maiden name," she puts in.

"Well goddamn it don't tell me his real name. In fact, don't tell me anything. I'm just... wow, I have no words. I thought you and I had something... I at least thought I had your respect, your consideration..." Grant stands up abruptly and heads back to the front door. He grabs his jacket off the coat-rack and with a sober "Goodnight, Judith" is out the door. Gone.

Judith bursts into tears. She'd hoped their night would end quite differently but it wouldn't matter if it didn't, not so long as she and Grant are still together. This stiff, angry, and hurt man is a stranger to her and she has no one to blame but herself. She cries bitterly.

Grant has walked several steps down the hall before he realizes he hasn't heard the sound he's been subconsciously listening for: the snap of the deadbolt locking into place. He turns back but then he hears Judith sobbing. Part of him wants to soothe away her tears but another part feels badly used, his trust shattered.

How can she care so little? Why has he let himself be fooled into thinking that... Grant isn't used to feeling indecisive. He stands in the hallway trying to piece together what he wants and what he should do.

He's exhausted from the late night and heartsick at the destruction he witnessed, and he knows he's not in the best place right now. He can't think clearly, he's too upset.

In the end he turns away from her door and continues to the stairs. Once he's hurried down to the ground floor he sends her a text saying:

'lock yr door'

Judith sees the text and runs out to the hallway but Grant is long gone. *He does care, he still cares!* is her wild thought until she realizes he was just reacting the way any cop would with any... civilian.

Chapter Twenty-Nine

Sunday, February 23, 2020

Judith is feeling listless, dull, and depressed. She's stayed in bed much later than usual and her muscles ache from lying down too long. Dragging herself into the kitchen she makes a cup of coffee she doesn't even feel like drinking. Food is out of the question.

Looking up at the clock she groans over how many stultifying hours she has to get through until she can reasonably go back to bed. Sundays are settling into a dreary pattern.

Grant doesn't want to speak to her, and neither does Lila who is in Toronto, anyhow. Now nobody is friendly, and everyone is unhappy.

Judith wonders if the onus is on her to apologize – but to whom and for what? Grant shouldn't expect her to reveal Lila's secret – she isn't a tattletale! and Lila shouldn't have demanded she keep a secret from Grant in the first place. It isn't a big stretch of the imagination to figure out it will come between them.

Judith feels sorry for herself, deciding it isn't fair for her two friends to put her in the middle with their demands and priorities. But it is hard to feel both justified and miserable at the same time.

She's heard the church bells and finds herself wishing she is one of the faithful but she hasn't grown up with religion. When she did learn about God she figured He'd forsaken her a long time ago. It's hard to overcome the absolutes of childhood – especially the self-taught truths.

Still, it would be nice to have somewhere to go today. She could have sang the hymns and listened to the sermon from the Reverend. Thinking of the Reverend makes her think of Rev Robbie... of course!

she can go to The Centre and make herself useful. She has her copy of the thumb-drive and from it she can reconstruct the finances up until Rev Robbie's death, and then work on getting it all straightened out. And arranging an off-site back-up, too. It feels good to have a plan, and good to have something useful to do.

Now Judith feels energized as she gets herself ready to go out. She has just hopped in the shower when someone knocks at her door but too quietly for her to hear over the spray of the water.

About twenty minutes later, dressed comfortably in jeans and a hoodie, Judith is locking her door when she is hit hard from behind. The force of that blow knocks her forehead into her own apartment door and Judith collapses, senseless, in her hallway. She has no idea who attacked her.

* * * * * *

Brian Penner is worried about Lila Morelli. He thinks he's done a good job of keeping his feelings for her hidden, but his daughter Bethany sees right through him. Beth has turned into a conscientious and empathetic girl. Brian is proud of the way she'd taken that Margaret Seely under her wing even though the girl is quite a bit younger. Smart though, and with a smart mouth, too, but Brian keeps that opinion to himself.

Beth has told her Dad that she's spoken to Ms. Taylor, the school bursar, about Margaret's mother leaving her alone so much.

"I don't like to be a rat or anything but Dad, Margaret's only nine. She's too young to be left alone overnight. The Seely's have money and if somebody noticed that only a child was in the house well, they might decide to rob the place."

"Yeah, well Miss Margaret Seely could give that *Home Alone* kid a run for his money if crooks tried to invade her place, don't you think?"

This makes Beth laugh. She and her father had watched that movie, again, this past Christmas. He is right about Margaret being clever and ingenious but nevertheless she is just a kid.

This morning, however, it's her Dad she is concerned about. When she asks him what's up and he tries hedging she steers him straight to the point:

"You're worried about Lila, aren't you?"

"No, not really. Well, maybe a little.. just a little bit anxious. She's been so bothered lately and just not herself."

"Well you know what Ms. Taylor said about Lila's husband coming out here and getting her upset."

"Yeah, she still hasn't talked to me about that but at least she did call to tell me she was going to Toronto sooner than planned and expected to get everything finally sorted out. I just wish I could help her somehow. You know, Beth, I'm very, uh fond of Lila. Even as more than a friend."

"I know, Dad, and I'm so happy about it. I think she's great."

That makes Brian grin as he agrees.

"I am worried about her though but I don't think it would be right for me to phone her. Not when she's in Toronto and not when she's working out whatever it is," he says.

"Well then, why don't you go talk to Ms. Taylor? Remember how she helped when I went missing?"

"Oh God, I'll never forget that time Bethie."

Hearing her childhood name makes Beth smile. She gives her father a hug and says she has Ms. Taylor's address from sending her a thank you card back in January so why doesn't he drop round to see if she can give him some news? or at least some reassurance?

Brian had cut back on his work hours after Beth was safely returned home but at times like this he wishes he had something to do and somewhere to go. He realizes sitting around moping and fretting isn't doing him any good so he agrees with his daughter's suggestion.

"Guess I better change out of these grubby old sweats, eh?"

"Uh, yeah, unless you want Ms. Taylor to tell Lila to run the other way!"

Taking Beth's advice is the reason that Brian Penner arrives to find Judith Taylor lying on the floor in front of her apartment with a woman rifling through her victim's purse.

Brian Penner is a big man, strong with a construction worker's muscles, and the sight of Judith lying unresponsive is all he needs to grab and subdue the attacker, Andrea Seely.

"Let me go," she shrieks, "She knows! she knows! and she must have some proof, I've *gotta* find the proof!"

Brian has seen Andrea Seely before but he doesn't recognize this maddened creature with her wild eyes and fingers curled into claws. He doesn't care how roughly he handles her as he pulls her arms behind her back and pushs her down to the floor. She twists and turns and yells but is no match for him. He half-kneels on her back to restrain her wildly struggling form. Holding her wrists together he uses his other hand to dial 9-1-1 on his cell-phone, requesting an ambulance and the police.

* * * * * *

Judith recovers consciousness during the ambulance ride but is admitted to the hospital for tests, then kept in overnight for observation. The medical staff are concerned about the severe blow she's taken to the back of her head.

She is bruised and shaky and has no memory of what happened since the moment she locked her door – in the middle of a Sunday afternoon.

Grant feels sick when he learns about the attack on Judith, and deeply dismayed that he wasn't the one to rescue her. He remembers Brian Penner from that case last December. He is a devoted dad and a well-built, good-looking, single man who had garnered the sympathy of both Lila and Judith.

Grant knows he should be glad that Penner was on the spot at the right time, but he isn't feeling grateful.

Chapter Thirty

Monday, February 24, 2020

Judith learns that when an ambulance brings you to the hospital it's up to you to find your own transportation when the time comes to return home. That's fine, except they won't let you go home in a taxi or an Uber, it has to be with someone who will see you safely indoors and stay with you.

Judith has patiently explained that no, there is no one at home because she lives alone. When the nurse repeats the regulation yet again Judith's patience runs out.

"For the umpteenth time I am a single woman who lives alone, no room-mate, no family, an orphan, no relatives. There is no one at home and there probably never will be!"

"Well, we need the bed and since you don't need it anymore you have to leave," replies the nurse.

Judith gives her a puzzled look saying "I don't want the bed, I *want* to leave. I want to go home."

"But as I've already explained," the nurse continues in an exaggeratedly patient voice, "You can't go home if there's no one there to look after you."

"Don't be ridiculous," snaps Judith. "I'm going home and I'll make my own travel arrangements since you won't help."

"I'm going to get my supervisor," threatens the nurse.

Exasperated Judith retorts: "Yes, you do that, just go."

"Well there's no need to be rude–" the nurse begins when Judith interrupts to say that apparently, there is.

While the nurse hurries away Judith retrieves her belongings from the bedside locker and checking that her cell-phone still has a charge calls Pat Johnson.

"Judith!" exclaims Pat, "Samira has just this minute been telling me about what happened to you. Beth Penner came in and told her. How are you? What happened? Where are you? Goodness I'm babbling, aren't I? Can I come see you?"

"Actually Pat I'm calling to see if Mark still does his volunteer driving for people needing to go to and from the hospital? They don't want to let me go home in a taxi. Some bloody stupid regulation they have."

"Oh poor Judith! I'll call Mark right away and he'll be waiting for you out front. I'll head over to your place now so you can tell the staff that someone is at your home."

"You don't have to do that, Pat, it's a school day and you're busy–"

"Never mind about that. I will see you shortly and you can tell me everything, or if you're exhausted I'll tuck you into your bed and leave you in peace."

"Thank you so much, Pat. I look forward to seeing you and finding out what actually happened to me."

Judith ends the call just as the nurse returns with her supervisor.

"I've arranged to be picked up and delivered into the care of Patricia Johnson, Principal of Edgemont School for Girls. I'm sure you'll agree she's capable enough of keeping an eye on me."

The supervisor, busy with more pressing issues, is thankful that everything is sorted and approves this plan. The nurse gives an almighty sniff of displeasure which Judith happily ignores.

She completes her paperwork and makes her way to the front door, relieved to escape the odor and atmosphere of the hospital. She only has to wait two minutes before spotting Principal Johnson's husband pull up in front in his blue sedan.

* * * * * *

Pat Johnson arrives at Judith's apartment and recognizing her husband's car she parks behind him. Mark and Judith have just reached the lobby so Pat takes over from there.

Once they are settled upstairs in Judith's apartment Pat makes a pot of tea and passes on all the information she has learned.

"You were attacked by Andrea Seely who, apparently, poisoned Rev Robbie with the drug Fentanyl. I have no idea how Andrea got hold of it–"

"She knew the combination to the safe," replied Judith and at Pat's quizzical look she explained: "This is only supposition but Grant.." she paused a moment remembering the look on Grant's face last night during the brief visit the nursing staff had allowed him, but she preferred to reminisce about that on her own so she continued: "Grant and I discussed this and we think Rev Robbie caught somebody with the drugs which he confiscated and locked in the safe out of harm's way."

"But surely he would notify the police?"

"Would he? if it was a young person who Rev Robbie felt could be turned around without getting a criminal record?"

"Ahhh, you're right. That scenario does sound likely."

"And anyone who knew the combination to the safe could get hold of the drugs themselves. Andrea Seely, as Treasurer, knew the combination."

"Well she's got a lawyer and isn't uttering a word now but Brian Penner got quite an earful from her, he rescued you, you know."

"I heard that, but I don't actually remember anything."

"No, well you were unconscious so not surprising!" laughs Pat. "Oh, I shouldn't laugh because she really did do some damage – have you seen your face?"

"I don't want to. I can feel a goose egg on the back of my skull and I've got what feels like a huge bandage on my forehead."

"Be glad it's not the other way around or they'd have had to shave off a patch of your hair."

"Oh, ewww!"

"I know, eh? Actually the bandage isn't too big but you do have a black eye and you're very pale so bit of a mess, I'm afraid, but you'll heal and that's the main thing."

"Okay so why did Andrea Seely do all this?"

"Well we don't know! In fact we're all hoping your policeman will tell you so you can tell us. Will he be coming by?"

"He said he would, but if he mentioned a time I've forgotten it."

"Maybe you should give him a call and let him know you're home now."

"Yes, I'll do that. Pat, I really appreciate you being here for me but I know you've got to get back to the school."

"Call the detective and we'll see if he can come by now." Pat fetches Judith's bag so she can get her mobile. She stares stupidly at the phone until Pat takes it from her saying:

"His name is Grant, right?"

Judith nods and listens while Pat conducts a very efficient phone-call with George Grant who says he'll be over right away.

"You just stay lying there on the couch and I'll wait to let him in when he gets here. I won't quiz him – tempting though that is! but when you're feeling better please give me a call and an update, okay?"

"Thanks, Pat."

The older woman smooths Judith's hair back from her forehead and finding an afghan folded over a chair she covers Judith up.

"Just close your eyes and nap, Judith."

Chapter Thirty-One

About an hour later, when Judith wakens, it's Grant sitting beside her holding her hand. She gives him a sweet smile to show how happy she is to see him, but he's looking anxious.

"Judith I am so, so sorry I wasn't there to protect you.. or at least to be the one to find you. Brian Penner, eh? Why was he even here?"

"I have no idea Grant," then noting his frown adds: "He's never been here before."

Grant's shoulders drop down, relaxing some of his tension, but his face still shows concern.

"How do you feel? Your poor head, all bandaged... Judith I feel awful about quarrelling with you–"

"Oh, don't. You were right, I should have told you. I felt my loyalties were torn between you and Lila but I did everything wrong and ended up making both of you mad at me."

"Why is Lila mad?"

"She feels I pushed her into this position of telling Arnie that he has to inform the authorities or she will."

"But that's the right thing – *the only thing* – to do."

"And she knows that, she even acknowledged it, but she still blames me."

"Well that's not fair. You only pushed to help her since she's been dithering about this for weeks. I re-interviewed her but had to cut our meeting short because she was so disconnected. She obviously needed like twelve hours of sleep! she couldn't focus well enough to answer my questions. I don't how long she would have continued but something would have snapped sooner or later."

"Yeah, Rev Robbie's death was like the final straw. Boy, that Arnie really did a number on her when he came out to visit."

"Didn't you or Lila mention, actually she mentioned at Christmas, that her family were all cops, right?"

"Not her immediate family, well a younger brother is in training or whatever. But not her Dad. However her uncles, some aunts, and her grandfather are all cops so, yeah she's got plenty in her family but I'd guess there's still a bit of an us-and-them attitude since neither of her parents are on the force."

"You're right, there would be. Both sides probably look down on each other a bit, privately of course, but yeah.

So what you're saying is that Lila blew you off and then I came over and basically did the same. Then you got your head bashed in."

"Pretty much! but I don't remember a thing about that. I was feeling pretty low that morning," Grant winces, recalling how he'd heard her sobbing when he left the night before, and she hastens to explain, "but I decided to do something positive, I was heading to The Centre with my thumb drive to see if I could help get the financials back on track.

I know Rev Robbie's computer was stolen, but there are plenty of other computers and lap-tops there. So, that was my plan and I was feeling better to actually be doing something when bang, I guess. I don't remember anything else until I came to in the ambulance.

I might remember more. I mean, Brian was there fighting with Andrea so subconsciously I must have been hearing things but I really don't care if that memory ever returns to be honest."

Grant leans over and kisses her forehead beside the bandage. Then he kisses her nose and when she smiles he bends to her lips and gives her a proper kiss.

"Why on earth would Andrea Seely want to harm you?"

Judith was surprised and struggled a bit to sit up: "You mean you don't know?"

"Do you?"

"No, not a clue."

"Me neither. Well, actually that's not quite true because we do have two clues. One is that according to Brian Penner Seely kept yelling 'she knows' and 'I've got to find her proof' which sure sounds like she thinks you knew something that's compromising to her. And two: our financial forensics specialist found evidence of theft and fraudulent entries on your thumb drive. No indication by whom, but based on what's just happened I think it's a safe bet that Andrea Seely, in her position as Treasurer, was misappropriating funds. They'll track it all down eventually.

The very first time I spoke to her she tried to cast the blame on Rev Robbie but you know she's such a silly and annoying woman that I have to admit I was guilty of dismissing her. I felt she was just trying to make herself look important. I won't make that mistake with her again. When I interview her I plan to ask about the money, The Centre's financial records, and of course why she attacked you."

"You know, Grant, she has been clever enough to play everyone. I was thinking on... I'm not sure, a couple of days ago anyhow, I thought that maybe her chasing the boy Kyle-something was just a smokescreen."

"You never mentioned any of this, I don't know what you mean?"

"Then you're one of the few people who doesn't know! Even her daughter – you remember precocious Margaret?"

"How could I forget her!"

"Well, Margaret got into a fist-fight at school because some older student repeated the rumour that's been going around about how Andrea Seely is chasing after the young sports coach, called Kyle, from The Centre. She's made a laughingstock of herself but what I got to thinking was: what if that was deliberate? What if Andrea played up to be this character people ridiculed and dismissed as cover for something else?"

"Like stealing The Centre's money? Maybe..." He paused to mull over this idea for a few moments before asking: "But why?"

"That is a mystery because you saw their home, it's a mansion. The Seely's are very well-off."

"Except that looks can deceive, right?"

"Oh sure, all flash no cash, but Pat confirmed that Mr. Seely – I can't remember his first name – is a very successful businessman. So this means you haven't interviewed Andrea Seely yet?"

"I tried but she lawyered up immediately, and the first thing her lawyer did was ask for a psych evaluation so now I'm cooling my heels till I get the all-clear."

"I'd like to think about this some more because I don't see how Andrea Seely and the drugs and Rev Robbie can connect but my head is a little fuzzy. Maybe I'll just close my eyes again for a bit..."

"Yes, do that. Get your rest, Judith. I'm not going anywhere," Grant reassures her.

He shifts their seats so that he can put his arm around her shoulders and lay her head against his chest. Judith snuggles into his embrace and her slowed breathing indicates she'd fallen asleep. Grant is careful not to let his chin drop down on her head since she is bruised and bandaged.

He is planning to think through all they've discussed but soon his eyes are closed, too. He didn't sleep well the night before.

* * * * * *

Judith wakes with her face pressed into Grant's shirt. She stays still for a moment listening to his heartbeat. He is stroking her arm and when she sits up he pulls her close for a slow, satisfying kiss. After an enjoyable interlude of kissing she draws back saying:

"I need coffee, food, and a pee."

"In that order?"

"Almost!" Freeing herself from his arms she heads to the bathroom. Grant stands up as well and stretches, his long legs have felt cramped caught between the coffee table and the couch but he didn't want to move and disturb her.

"I doubt if you want to go out for a meal," he says when Judith returns, "so what would you like me to order in?"

"Nothing," she replies. "If you don't mind I'm craving chicken noodle soup and a grilled cheese sandwich."

"Oh, wow, that sounds great!" he says with enthusiasm.

"Well, it's just tinned soup but it's comfort food and I enjoy it every now and then."

"Can I help? I'm an expert can opener..."

"No, there's not enough room in my kitchen for both of us but you can sit at the table and keep me company. First though, when we mentioned Margaret before you didn't tell me who is looking after her now while her mother's in custody?"

"She's staying with the Penners until her father gets back. We were able to get hold of him and he's probably already here by now. His name is John, by the way, John Seely. He was quite forthcoming with me, although shocked when he heard about the assault on you.

It seems Andrea was making it difficult for him to see Margaret – who is reportedly thrilled to be with her Dad. Andrea was withholding access in order to get more money from him. Anyhow, Margaret is being looked after.

But the important question is how are you feeling? and be honest!"

"I think I'm always honest, Grant. In fact, I've been told I'm *honest to a fault.* So I'm telling you the truth when I say you that although I'm a bit weak I'm not the least bit headachey – which is a surprise considering I just saw how bad my battered face looks in the bathroom mirror."

"You can never look bad to me, Judith."

The two are comfortable with each other and when Judith brings out plates and cutlery Grant sets the table. They drink their coffee while she cooks and in fifteen minutes are having their soup and sandwiches.

"So, any insights while you were napping?" asks Grant.

"Yes, as a matter of fact. It occurred to me that Andrea either moved really fast to seize the opportunity of Rev Robbie's death to clean out the safe, or, she'd emptied it already. If so, did she leave it open? is that why the Fentanyl was available to his killer? and what were the dates that the funds were stolen? That must have happened very close to the murder or Rev Robbie would have raised the alarm."

"I think Andrea Seely killed Rev Robbie."

"I realize she must have done, Pat said so too, but it's truly a shocker. I mean, I can imagine her stealing well, no I can't actually imagine that because it makes no sense, but murder? That's a huge leap from theft!"

"I agree, but it's my only conclusion. Here's my thinking:

Andrea Seely, for whatever reason, is going through large amounts of money. She's been elected or appointed Treasurer at The Centre which gives her access to the cash in the bank account. She also has the combination to the safe where the daily collections are stored. She transfers or withdraws the banked funds, and helps herself to the loose cash in the safe.

Rev Robbie either catches her in the act or accuses her. She makes up some story to buy a bit of time – but probably just a day at most – then arranges to meet with him to be counselled, or to discuss a repayment plan, or something like that. She has nothing to do with the drugs except that she's seen the Fentanyl in the safe or, somehow, knows it's there and she steals it.

I'm guessing that when she meets with Rev Robbie she arrives with coffees or more likely chai lattes knowing her, and she's doctored his. She probably used all of the Fentanyl because we only found the tiniest amount left behind. It's a highly potent drug and he dies quickly.

She's picked a time when there are lots of people about, especially young people who she hopes will fall under suspicion because of the drug angle, and that's why she left the safe open, too."

"Wow, that answers all the questions. Good work, Grant."

"It doesn't explain why she stole the money in the first place, though."

"Oh that's easy, Andrea Seely has a gambling problem."

"That would explain it... but how do you know?"

"Well I don't *know* but Lila and I saw her at the casino when we went for dinner with those tickets you gave me."

"Okay, but lots of people go to casinos. It doesn't mean they have an addiction and are stealing to feed their habit."

"True, but what about all her absences? Margaret is left at home alone a lot and even when her mother's there she often slips out late at night after Margaret's gone to bed. The casinos are open very late, aren't they?"

"Yes, they are and seven days a week. Judith, I think you might be on to something. There have been several cases in the last few years where gamblers – all women, actually – were caught embezzling large amounts of money from their employers and their defence was an addiction to slot machines and VLTs."

"What are those?"

"Video Lottery Terminals, a kind of slot machine."

"Oh. Did the embezzlers get off?"

"God no, they've all been convicted and either fined or jailed, and ordered to pay back the money. So far that defence has never been successful."

"Maybe that's what's caused the breakdown of her marriage? maybe her husband knew about the gambling and cut off the funds."

"We're not sure about the gambling–"

"I am," Judith insists, "And if Andrea won't talk maybe John Seely will? Maybe he's had enough of his wife and her using Margaret as a pawn to get more money out of him."

"We'll find out more when I actually get her into an interview room. At the moment we've only got her on assault. Oh, you will press charges, right?"

"Absolutely. Hey, it's becoming a bit of a habit with me... first Billy MacNeill and now Andrea Seely."

"I'll bet she's the one who broke into your car and stole The Centre's bookkeeping ledger. Especially if she has been looking for some sort of proof. As a parent she'd have a pretty good idea of the school routines and could pick the best time to do it unseen.

But since nothing was pointing the finger at her, specifically, why did she keep saying *she knows, she knows* to Brian Penner?"

"Oh that must be because of... oh, that's my fault. After Margaret got suspended for fighting Andrea demanded a meeting, the silly woman thought she could bully Pat into letting Margaret come back to class. I was present and she made some remark or something, damn that's something else I can't remember. Anyhow, I was annoyed, especially knowing that she kept leaving Margaret alone which might not be illegal but it's morally reprehensible. So I phoned but I got the answering machine and I had to be circumspect in how I worded my message in case Margaret heard. Andrea must have thought I was hinting and beating around the bush... oh, her guilty conscience filled in the blanks!"

They finish their meal and sit over another cup of coffee.

"Despite all this caffeine and my nap I think I'm going to have an early night," says Judith.

"I'm staying over," insists Grant. He notes her sudden blush and quickly adds: "On the couch. I just don't want to leave you alone, Judith."

"Thank you, Grant. That's very kind and reassuring, too. By the way, if Fentanyl is so deadly why is it available?"

"It's one of those products that turned out to be so much better than the hype! It's just about the best painkiller hospitals can use, about thirty times more powerful than heroin. So it comes into the country legally for medical use but too often it ends up in the hands of drugs dealers and their clients. It's caused a lot of deaths because it's easy to overdose."

"Oh, I wondered. I've never experimented with any kind of drugs, never had a sip of wine or beer or alcohol, and never smoked a cigarette. Pretty dull and boring life, eh?"

Grant stares into her eyes and she is drawn by the sparkling interest she sees in his. *Oh! He must have realized I haven't had any sexual experiences either!* Judith feels the heat of her blush flooding her cheeks and quickly glances away.

"I don't think you're boring or dull at all, Judith. But you know, you should probably get in touch with the Red Cross because I'll bet they'd love to have you as a Blood Donor."

Judith laughs, his comment having rescued her from embarrassment, and the tension that's built-up between them breaks harmlessly.

"I tried to give blood once but they wouldn't take it. There was a clinic set up for two days at the University and when the nurse said I looked pale and asked if I was sick I said *oh no, it's just my* oh! maybe I shouldn't, oh what the heck you said you've got sisters so I'm sure you know all about it... anyhow I said I was on *my period* so she said I couldn't. I later learned that's wrong and I could have donated, but I've never tried again. You're right though, I should. It's something we should all do if we can."

"Do you know your blood type?"

"A+, you?"

"A-, one of the rarer types. I can give blood to you but I can't take it from you. I can only receive blood from A- and O-. No B types."

"Same, I can't take blood from B types but the others are okay. So, we're somewhat compatible?"

Gathering up their used coffee cups Grant turns to the sink calling over his shoulder:

"I think we're very compatible, Judith. Now, let's get you to bed."

Chapter Thirty-Two

True to his word Grant stays on the couch all night but in the morning Judith wakens to find him sitting on the edge of her bed. He's looking at her like she's a beautiful woman, and his look makes her feel like she really is. Without a word she opens her arms to him and then he's holding her, kissing her, and murmuring lovely words. The rest just happens naturally.

Judith has left him to start coffee and toast while she gets cleaned up. She's not yet ready for company in the shower, especially since she has to wear a shower cap to keep her head dry. *I wish I could wash my hair,* she thinks, *but that's a no-no right now.*

When she comes out of the bathroom, fully dressed but in comfortable clothes, he tells her her phone's been ringing and buzzing so she has a look and see missed calls and a *call me now* text from Pat Johnson.

"It's my boss sounding urgent so I'd better phone her right away," she says, hitting the button. Pat answers immediately:

"Judith, thank God! I need to tell somebody but there's nobody else I can really tell. Well, Samira, of course, but you need to know."

"Know what, Pat?"

"It's Lila! She just called me from Toronto. Judith, her husband has committed suicide! He's dead! Suicide! Can you believe it? Did you meet him when he was out here? I know he visited at the beginning of the year..."

"No, I didn't. We planned to but... omigod Pat, this is just awful, awful news."

Grant is staring at Judith with concern and she wants to tell him but doesn't want Pat to know he's still here so early in the day. Instead she just repeats the words:

"I can't believe Arnie has killed himself," and sees Grant's eyes widen in surprise just as a look of disgust crosses his face. "Poor Lila. What's she going... what are her plans?"

"Well first off, she is coming back so that's a huge relief. Apparently she has to stay over Saturday night to get a good price on her airfare–"

"What about the airline's bereavement discount? does she know about that?"

"Well it's really not much for domestic flights. Usually the sale price is better. Of course if it's an international flight then it really makes a difference... oh why are we talking about this?"

"Because the news is just so horrible we want to avoid thinking about it. Anyhow, does that mean she's coming back on Sunday?"

"Yes, the funeral is on Friday. They have to wait until then because the Coroner had to agree to release the body. Oh, Judith you're right, this is horrible. Anyhow, Lila's catching the first flight out on Sunday and we'll see her at school on Monday. Judith, Lila didn't say why Arnie did this and I couldn't very well ask her, but do you have any idea?"

"I might... but, I'm not sure. He's same age as Lila – and me – but I think there was a health thing or something. I was supposed to meet him but Lila and I didn't really talk much about his actual visit... I can't say for sure, Pat."

"Well, it's a very sad thing no matter what the reason behind it is."

"Yes, it is. Pat thanks for letting me know. Toronto time is two hours ahead of us, right? I'll call her now–"

"Oh Judith, Lila asked that I pass on her news because she doesn't want to talk to anyone herself."

"Oh! Okay, then. Well, still, thanks for telling me. Bye for now."

"Bye, Judith – oh wait, how are you feeling today? Better?"

Judith has been looking at Grant throughout her conversation. "I was feeling great until I got this news. Physically I feel... wonderful, thanks!"

She disconnects the call and he pulls her straight into his arms.

"I only heard half of that and it was bad, tell me what's going on."

"Arnie has committed suicide, no explanation from Lila why, she doesn't want to talk to anybody, the funeral is Friday and she's flying back on Sunday morning. She plans to come to school on Monday so that must mean she's going to stay, right? She's not just coming back to wrap things up here?"

"Well, I don't know, Judith. But I don't think she'd rush back just to quit her job, break her lease, and plan a move, do you?"

"No, you're right. She'd stay with her family and get most of it sorted out long-distance. I should call her. I know things didn't end well between us but... either she hates me even more or she needs my comfort. I have to try."

"Okay, but remember she'll be really hurting right now and might say things that are... well, meant to hurt you back. You have to be the strong one, right?" He gives her a hug that turns into a long kiss.

Judith finds Lila's number in her contacts and calls. Lila doesn't answer and Judith can't leave a message because the mailbox is full. She tries again, several times, but never gets a different result.

Later, lying in each other's arm, Judith confesses to Grant:

"I feel doubly guilty now. One, because I can't help but see Arnie's death as probably the easiest solution to Lila's dilemma which isn't a very kind thought; and two because I'm feeling so happy here with you."

"I'm glad you feel that way, Judith. I was worried that you might feel overwhelmed by the news. I have no sympathy with suicides, they do terrible things to the people they leave behind."

"I expect I would have felt differently if Arnie and Lila had been a happy couple. Then I'd be devastated for her loss but–"

"I know what you mean. This way there's no trial, no family shame, no torn-apart loyalties. I'm guessing he did it before telling the authorities, don't you think? that's usually the way since cowards don't want to face up to their actions and the consequences."

"Yes, I think he did it instead of telling the authorities. You realize Lila is going to blame herself for driving him to it. Oh, she's going to blame me even more for pushing her..."

"But you said she was going to tell her family, at least her non-police relatives so that would be her parents, right? before giving Arnie the ultimatum?"

Judith sits up, animated by her thoughts: "Yes, that's right! She wanted him to know that there was no way he could talk her round, that it wasn't just their secret because she'd already told her parents. Yes! they would have backed her up in her decision. They're a close family and their support would definitely have fortified her. So I'm not entirely to blame..." she sighs with relief then sinks back into Grant's embrace.

Chapter Thirty-Three

Wednesday, February 26, 2020

Judith has to go back to the hospital on Wednesday for a check-up. The Resident she sees isn't happy with the state of her healing, saying the swelling should have gone done much more. He sends her for yet more tests. Judith feels a twinge of unease but consoles herself with the thought that Resident's are overly cautious, determined to dot every 'i' and cross every 't'.

She mentions that after getting bad news about a friend she hasn't been sleeping too well. He admonishes her that she needs to get her rest, it's an important part of healing. Judith smiles to herself thinking that the time she's been spending in bed lately isn't exactly restful... although it does feel healing.

She sends Grant a text knowing she'll be spending several hours at the hospital with her phoned switched off. Hoping he'll get it and reply right away she is delighted to hear the *ding!* of an incoming message. He wants to know if there is a problem and she replies:

JUDITH: no just tests

Grant goes on to say that Andrea Seely's lawyer has called and they are all meeting for an interview at 11:00 this morning. Judith wishes him good luck and ends the chat advising she'll check in as soon as she's finished, and can turn her phone back on again.

A couple of hours later, while waiting for test results, she spots Mark Johnson. Meeting up with him in the foyer she asks if he'll let her buy him a cup of coffee in thanks for the ride home he gave her on Monday.

"Oh no need for that, Ms. Taylor–" he begins, but Judith interrupts saying:

"Judith, please. And I'd like to have a coffee myself. In fact, I see this hospital has a mini Tim Horton's concession and I could go for a doughnut, too."

He smiles and agrees, giving her his order and saying he'll grab a table for them.

Minutes later Judith joins him at a high-top carrying a tray holding their drinks and snacks.

"Let's see, this is yours since the mug is marked Decaf," she says, passing it over to him. Sitting back to sip their hot drinks and take a bite of doughnut, Judith continues: "This is a busy hospital, isn't it? Is this the only one you drive for?"

"I mostly get calls for here, the Villages Hospital, because it's close to my home and I can get here fairly quickly, but I have been asked to take people to and from Calgary hospitals as well. I've been getting more calls than usual lately. Lots of people suffering bad cases of the flu."

"Well, I think it's a great service you provide, Mr. Johnson. I know I certainly appreciated it. I was beginning to think that nurse was going to keep me here!"

He chuckles at that, adding: "They love their policies, don't they? How did you get here today?"

"I drove myself... it never occurred to me that maybe I shouldn't? I feel fine, no faintness, headaches, or ringing in my ears. I just seem to tire more quickly than before but I'm sure I'll soon have my strength back."

They sit in companionable silence, eating and sipping.

"Normally I enjoy people-watching when I'm on the sidelines like this but a hospital is different, isn't it?"

"Yes, I understand what you're saying. It's different at airports and shopping centres because people might be rushed and harried but, for the most part, they're happy to be there. Whereas here, well nobody wants to be here except the staff."

"I guess they get used to the smell over time."

"What smell?" asks Mark Johnson with a sly smile.

Judith's name is paged so she gets up to head back to her section. Mark Johnson thanks her for the coffee, and she thanks him again for her ride and for keeping her company today.

This time the Resident is accompanied by a middle-aged doctor who explains that the amount of swelling is normal for the severity of the blow and the slow healing isn't a worry. The Resident had been concerned in case chips of bone had come loose which is why he brought it to her attention but she tells Judith there is no indication of anything like that.

"The scans show heavy bruising that goes down deep so the blow you took was harder than we originally realized. Based on that we've determined that the pace of your healing is normal, and you need to to stay off work for a few more days to get well-rested."

"When can I wash my hair?"

"Not yet, I'm afraid. But it doesn't look bad, you know, it's not greasy-looking." The doctor, whose own hair is pulled into a perfect french twist, has a good look and adds: "In another day or two you can try a dry shampoo but keep it away from the abraded area, okay?"

The Resident changes Judith's dressing then escorts her to the Out-Patients reception to make a follow-up appointment for Monday.

Back in her own car Judith switches on her phone to check for messages. Just the one, from Grant, saying the interview with Andrea Seely has been delayed until 3:00. The car clock reads 4:10 and out of habit Judith automatically checks the time on her phone to confirm it matches. It does.

Judith texts back her own message saying she's finally finished up at the hospital and everything is good. She plans to go straight home but *en route* changes her mind and instead drives to the Penner residence. She is curious, though very grateful, about why Brian Penner came to her apartment building on Sunday.

"By time I get there Beth should have gotten home from school," she spoke aloud. "And even if her Dad isn't home from work yet, she'll probably know why he came round to my place."

It's a short drive from the hospital to their home. Edgemont isn't a large village – just a wealthy one.

Brian Penner's not home yet but Beth is there and she welcomes Judith. The bungalow is homey and lived-in, with a bookmarked novel on the arm of an overstuffed chair, nail polish paraphernalia set out beside an open magazine on the coffee table, a sweater hanging from a doorknob... Judith figures they must have a cleaner come in on a weekly basis.

"I heard about what happened, Ms. Taylor. Look at your poor head! you're all bruised, too."

Judith refuses a hot drink, explaining she's had a coffee and doughnut at the hospital, but Beth's offer of a ginger-ale is appealing.

"Yes, I'll have a glass of that, thanks. Ginger-ale always makes me think of drinking it to get better, same with chicken noodle soup."

"Me, too!" exclaims Beth. "But other than the bruises and that big bandage you really don't look sick."

"No, I'm not. I'm a little tired, that's all, so I won't stay, but I did want to ask your father why he came over to my apartment and, of course, to thank him for saving me. Did you know it was Andrea Seely, Margaret's mother, who attacked me?"

"Omigod yes! Everybody's talking about it but nobody can believe it. Everyone thought she was just so... Anyhow, I met Margaret's Dad when he came by here to take her home and he's a really nice man. She'd been staying with us, you know."

"Yes, I heard."

"Well, it was a pretty upsetting time for her I mean first you get attacked and then it turns out it was by her mother! But once her Dad arrived everything was okay. Margaret had really been missing her father and he took her straight back to their own home, no hotel this time, so she's settled again.

I know she'll be glad to hear that you're up and about, too. She was worried about you... and worried about you not liking her any more."

"No, really? That's silly, Margaret's not responsible for her mother's actions." Judith thinks about her words and, as usual these past couple of days, her mind immediately travels to what happened with Arnie, and to Lila, and their friendship.

"Beth, have you heard anything about Ms. Morelli?"

"I heard she'll be back at school on Monday but that's all I know."

"Hmmm. Well, you can tell your Dad about this but no one else, okay?" Judith pauses to get Beth's agreement before continuing: "Lila's husband has.. well, he's killed himself. He's dead and Lila is now a widow. Committing suicide is a truly awful thing to do and she's going to be feeling very fragile. I just thought you should know."

"He killed himself? but he's old, I mean if he and Lila were married then he's gotta be like my Dad's age! I thought only teenagers killed themselves?"

"Well we don't know why he did it but..."

"Probably because she said she wasn't coming back, don't you think?"

"Well that's... possible. That would be a more likely reason for a teenage suicide but still... yeah, it could be. Anyhow, I don't want us to dwell on that, but I did think you and your Dad should know. Anyhow, Beth, your Dad might have saved my life, he's a hero."

"I know! I've always known that, though," smiles Beth. "And I'm kinda proud of myself too, see, 'cause I'm the one who made him go round to see you. If he hadn't well... who knows what would have happened?"

"What do you mean?"

"Dad really likes Lila – and I mean *really* likes Lila – so ever since she shut us out he's been moping around. When we found out that she went back to Toronto now instead of waiting until Easter he figured something was wrong or well... I 'm not sure what he thought, but anyhow I told him he should ask you. Do you know why she suddenly went back?"

"I have some ideas but I don't want to speculate. So you suggested your father come round to my place to ask if I knew what was going on with Lila?"

"Yes, that's right. You don't mind, do you?"

"In view of what happened? I'm thrilled he was there. Otherwise, well... yeah I guess it was okay. We do have to look after the men, don't we?"

The two smile at each other as if they are worldly-wise women. Judith finishes her drink and stands to go asking Beth to pass on what they've discussed to her father, including her thanks.

"I'll get your Dad a bottle of something, what type of liquor does he drink?"

"Scotch. Single malt but I think that's expensive so..."

"A bottle of single malt Scotch it is, then. Thanks, Beth. I expect I'll be back at school on Monday so will see you then."

Chapter Thirty-Four

Wednesday, February 26, 2020

At 9:00 am Grant meets with the lawyer from the Crown Prosecutor's office to discuss strategy. He is ready well in advance of the 11:00 o'clock appointment when he gets the call about a delay until mid-afternoon. Since he has nothing else scheduled, having planned on being in an interview room, he decides to take a chance on getting hold of John Seely, Andrea's estranged husband.

"Mr. Seely is away from the office but will be picking up messages if you care to leave one?" says John Seely's P.A. Grant's call has been transferred three times to get this far and his renowned patience is wearing thin. Of course he hasn't said he is from the police, the matter only affects Seely indirectly so no point in causing talk, but he isn't willing to wait any longer.

"Yes, thank you, this is in relation to a family matter of Mr. Seely's so please have him contact Detective George Grant–" Seely's assistant interrupts to say she is aware of the incident involving Mrs. Seely and, as instructed, will give Grant Mr. Seely's cell number so he can reach him directly.

Grant thanks her again and makes the call. John Seely invites Grant to come over to his house for lunch saying:

"My cooking skills are pretty much limited to omelettes but if that works for you..."

"That sounds great, yes. I know roughly where your house is but I don't have the exact address."

John Seely gives it to him then mentions that "Margaret's been allowed to return to class but I've kept her home from school this week while things get sorted out. It's not a problem though, I've also spoken very frankly with her because, well... I can't get away with anything else."

"I've met Margaret so yes, I understand."

"Oh you're *that* policeman... Margaret developed quite a crush! Now I'm really looking forward to meeting you Detective Grant!"

Grant is greeted by Margaret on his arrival and dragged through to the kitchen. The house has an ultramodern design and furnishings to match in numerous shades of gray. Grant feels right at home.

They eat a delicious meal and Grant is interested to see how Margaret see-saws between joy at being with her father then glumness when thinking about her mother's situation.

"You and I are probably on different sides of the fence here, Detective. I want Andrea to be sent to a rehab facility to deal with her gambling problem and that means getting her off this assault charge. I know that she'll be incarcerated if convicted but what she really needs is treatment."

"Her addiction isn't a defence–" begins Grant but is interrupted by John Seely saying:

"Agreed, but then we're probably going to dispute the whole assault claim."

"I've seen the victim, I know her, and she most definitely was assaulted."

"Hmm, your knowing her might compromise the impartiality of your involvement in this case, Detective."

Grant sits back and surveys the man, acknowledging his intelligent and ruthless grasp of the point.

"I discussed this with the Crown Prosecutor's Office, just this morning as a matter of fact, and the decision is that since I'm the lead investigator in the Reverend Robert Wilcox murder – which overlaps – then I'll at least do the interview."

John Seely is quiet for a moment as the implications of this new information sink in. He shoots a sideways glance at his daughter who is all ears.

"Margaret, my love–" he starts but is met by the nine-year-old stubbornly shaking her head and refusing to leave the room.

"I don't care what you have to say, Daddy. It doesn't matter. I know all about what Mother did to Ms. Taylor and I know she hated Rev Robbie. Everyone else loved him but she complained and complained that he was too nosey and too sharp—"

"Margaret stop!" insists her father cutting off further comment.

Grant stands saying:

"Don't worry, Mr. Seely. Margaret's comments are hearsay and inadmissible. I wasn't sure how much you knew and well... you're right, we're on opposite sides so I'll get going."

"I don't know whether or not our marriage can be salvaged out of all this but Margaret here needs both her parents and I want both of us to be here for her."

There's a hint of defiance in his tone but Grant simply nods, saying: "Thank you agreeing to see me, sir. And thank you for a very tasty lunch."

Grant checks his phone as soon as he leaves the house but no message yet from Judith. At least there isn't a message from Andrea Seely's lawyer about yet another delay.

Chapter Thirty-Five

Thursday, February 27, 2020

"Well the verdict's in on Andrea Seely and yup, she's crazy."

"Ahhh, an insanity plea. That's what came out from her psych evaluation?"

"Oh no, that's just my opinion."

Judith gives Grant a swat on the arm saying:

"Stop! this is serious stuff."

He pulls her close for a quick cuddle before continuing.

"No, I mean it. This afternoon? She had everything going her way with her high-priced lawyer, the expensive professional witness, and her well-connected husband, but she flipped out and couldn't or wouldn't stop talking. She was practically foaming at the mouth by the time she finished her tirade.

Actually, I think the lawyer will switch from the addiction defence to dissociative mental disorder, or psychotic break, or whatever the latest version of *temporary insanity* is called these days."

"What happened?"

"Well, we finally get everybody sitting down in the interview room which was like a game of Musical Chairs what with all the shuffling and stalling and nonsense.

I start laying out our case and all of a sudden she starts yelling – shrieking and swearing, actually – that I've got it all wrong. She started spitting out the words so fast it was impossible to understand. It took me half-a-dozen listens of the recording to even get the gist of what she was saying. Let's see, it was:

Rev Robbie was a liar who was trying to defame her because he *knew* she was only *borrowing* the money and that's why she had to kill him. The school accountant – I'm guessing that's you – was trying to threaten her, or maybe blackmail her or extort money, and all over a misunderstanding – I have no idea what that means – and she was only trying to get the proof back when she accidentally killed you, as she thinks.

And let's see... oh yeah, her husband has cut off her allowance, blocked her from the bank accounts, and refuses to give her any money even though she needs money to raise Margaret. Everyone hates her, they're all jealous, oh and my personal fav she's figured out a pattern to the slot machines and if everybody will just leave her alone to do her thing she is going to hit it big and bust the casino."

"Wow. She said a lot."

"And pretty much all in one sentence. The only time she paused was to draw in a deep enough breath to keep going. And she was loud too, because she was struggling to make herself heard over everyone else trying to shut her up."

"What do you think about her using this insanity defence?"

Grant sobers up as he thinks for a moment before replying: "This afternoon I did feel like I was sitting across the table from a crazy woman."

"This confession she made about killing Rev Robbie–"

"Yeah, it's on tape and her lawyer was right beside her, trying to put a lid on it, and the psychiatrist-for-the-defence can be heard talking over her, but she said certainly said the words."

"What do you think will happen to her?"

"I think she'll be spending a few years under psychiatric care and I believe that's the right outcome. If her husband gets his way it will be an expensive, private clinic. If the Crown wins its case she'll be moved to the public healthcare system.

Maybe John Seely will quietly divorce her and relocate with Margaret to a new city, or maybe he still loves Andrea. I couldn't get a read on his feelings about her. Regardless, he is devoted to his daughter so she'll be well taken care of."

"You know Grant, that's two murders I've been peripherally involved with and in both cases the killers were insane, crazy, mentally unfit..."

"Well Judith my love, I think anybody who kills is mentally unfit. I've been in law enforcement for a long time and while I'd advocate for rehabilitation for most crimes, I do believe that some people do need to be locked away for the safety of everyone else."

"Did Andrea Seely have anything to say about where the Fentanyl came from?"

"No, but she knew about it because of something Kyle Danby let slip. Poor guy was trying to get away from her and blurted out that Rev Robbie needed him to witness how much Fentanyl he was locking in the safe. By the way, I'm sure you're right about her pretending to lust after that young man as a distraction."

"So Kyle does know the source of the drug?"

"He says not, and I believe him. I'm pretty sure he has his suspicions but he won't incriminate anyone. Especially now that we can link that Fentanyl to the fatal dose Rev Robbie was given.

It doesn't matter that the person who brought the Fentanyl to The Centre never planned on it being taken away from them and used as a murder weapon but that's what happened so, arguably, they share some culpability."

"That's hardly fair—"

"But it was their deliberate actions that resulted in a murderer getting his/her hands on the deadly drug. You can't help but wonder if Rev Robbie would be dead if the poison hadn't been available.

Anyhow, nobody's going to own up to being the original owner of the Fentanyl now.

Meanwhile, you need to get your rest so that swelling can go down and your wound can heal. Your bruises are just beginning to blossom so you'll have them for a few days. People will probably give me funny looks."

"Beth gave me a funny look when I saw her today."

"Beth? was she at the hospital?"

"No, I detoured over to her place – actually to see her father – when I left the hospital. I knew she'd be home from school but wasn't sure if he'd be home from work. He wasn't, but she was able to answer my question about why he was here on Sunday.

Turns out she told him to come and talk to me. He was anxious about Lila, especially since she changed her plans to go to Toronto now instead of at Eastertime. Luckily for me he listened to Beth and did come over and right in the nick of time.

Grant, Andrea might have kept hitting me when she didn't find this proof she was looking for. That's a scary thought."

"It is, so don't think about it any more."

"But Andrea Seely must really be sick, eh?"

"Judith don't you dare feel sorry for that woman! She stole and when caught she murdered to cover up her crime. She was negligent about her daughter, and she attacked you. She doesn't deserve anyone's pity, least of all yours."

"No, you're right. She killed a very good and worthy man. And, now that I think of it, she was careful enough not to wear perfume when she did so or we'd have smelled it in his poky little office."

"That's true. It definitely was a premeditated killing, and she came to your place with the intention of doing you harm."

"Oh, that reminds me. I asked Beth what her father liked to drink and she said single malt Scotch. I've never been inside a liquor store and I'm really not keen to start now... will you buy this bottle for me? Of course I'll give you the money. I seem to remember my mother saying they only take cash."

"Judith, of course I'll buy the Scotch for Brian Penner and I will definitely pay for it. I'm the one who's grateful for his timely intervention. I've reaped all the benefits!"

"That's very kind of you but honestly I can afford to buy the bottle."

"I'm sure you can but please, let me do this for you."

"Okay, but you've already bought me the most beautiful earrings in the world and... well, you've done so much for me, Grant."

"Oh Judith, there's so much more to come."

Chapter Thirty-Six

Sunday, March 1, 2020

Judith is grateful for Grant's offer to go with her to meet Lila's plane but she wonders if she wouldn't be better off going on her own even though that would be a challenge.

"She might totally snub me and just walk right by," explains Judith.

"All the more reason for me to come along to comfort you," he replies.

"But maybe the sight of the two of us, together, will make her feel worse?"

"Then I'll wait in the car. Tell Lila that I'm just there as the chauffeur so that the two of you can concentrate on your conversation."

"That actually... that's a good idea. We can sit together and talk without the hassle of figuring out how to get out of the airport again and back here."

"It will give you and Lila a good chance to talk. And, if things don't work out well then, I'll be there for you, Judith."

* * * * * *

It's always nice to be welcomed by a familiar face in the crowd. Coming down the escalator Lila spots Judith pacing back and forth while looking around anxiously. It occurs to Lila that her friend might never have been inside an airport before, reminding herself that Judith lives a very restricted, solitary life.

But Lila doesn't feel ready to meet with anyone today, especially not Judith. She's all knotted up inside with painful, conflicting emotions *and I'm just beat*, she thinks to herself. *I don't want to talk at all. Not to anyone.*

Judith turns around and that's when Lila sees the large white bandage covering the top side of her forehead. Both eyes are bruised with one being extremely dark, and her skin looks so pale, her face so pinched. Lila immediately feels concern for her friend wondering what on earth has happened? A car accident? a serious fall? a mugging?

Just then Judith finds Lila and her face lights up with delight. Lila's response comes right from her core and it's an answering joy, realizing that the two of them really do care about each other. She waves and laughs to see Judith bouncing on the balls of her feet in anticipation. They meet in a hug so tight that the next passengers just move around instead of trying to interrupt.

Then both of them are speaking at the same time, interrupting each other:

"Lila! it's so good to see you—"

"It was really nice of you to come pick me up—"

"Grant drove, I've never been to the airport before, but he's told me we can ignore him and just talk to each other."

Judith carries Lila's bag so her friend can get into her outdoor things. Spring hasn't arrived in Calgary yet although the temperatures are ping-ponging between well-below and well-above seasonal averages. There is no chinook warming the air today but at least there's no snow, although that can change quickly.

As soon as they come through the sliding doors Grant pulls up to the curb. He hops out and gives Lila a quick hug before putting her case in the front seat and opening the back door for the women to slide in.

"I'm sorry for your loss, Lila, but it's good to see you back home again," he says.

"Thank you, Grant, and thanks for the ride, too."

"Well, it would be irresponsible of me to let Judith drive while bawling her eyes out so..." He gets back in his seat and drives off just as a traffic warden heads towards them.

Judith sees a forest of signs and is glad she doesn't have to read them while trying to steer the car out of the one-way system. Grant drives confidently so she is able to concentrate on Lila.

The strain of the past days – weeks, actually – show in lines and tension around Lila's eyes and mouth. Judith's own mouth trembles and without thinking a moment further both women collapse amid tears in each other's arms. They sob, hiccup, and laugh at themselves. They stay wrapped up in each other, giggling, apologizing, and mildly arguing, for the whole drive.

"What's with this bandage? what happened to you?"

"I was attacked by Andrea Seely, Margaret's mother, can you believe that?"

"But why?"

"Omigod you don't know... Andrea Seely killed Rev Robbie!"

"No! that BITCH! I could kill her myself. Hey Grant? pretend you didn't hear me say that!"

"Say what, Lila?"

"Why did she kill him? and why would she attack you?"

"Because she thought I knew something – which I didn't – but he did know that she was embezzling money from The Centre."

"She killed a fine man like that over money?"

"Worse, we think she killed him to protect her reputation. Everything I know about Rev Robbie makes me think he would have helped her repay the debt – over time or something – but he'd insist on making the Board aware of the situation, right? as part of her penitence or something. He'd help her but he wouldn't let her get off scot-free."

"No, he definitely wouldn't. He believed in the importance of facing up to mistakes. For Rev Robbie acknowledging and atoning would go hand-in-hand. Wow, this is hard to believe. But her husband is rich, why did she have to steal?"

"Andrea Seely has a gambling problem. She's poured a fortune into slot machines until her husband finally cut off the funds. Now, either she downplayed her problem or he didn't really believe in it, I don't know which, but he thought she would just stop playing once there was no more money. Instead, she stole and then killed to cover up her crime."

"Plus she attacked you–"

"And basically abandoned her daughter, too. Margaret was being left alone a lot – even late at night."

"She was spending a lot of time with the Penners'–"

"It was Brian Penner who save me from her."

"What? Brian?"

"Yeah, he's really got a thing for you, you know." Judith smiles as her friend suddenly gets an evasive look but then returns her stare saying,

"I thought so, and I had to ward him off. I knew my marriage was over, but while I was still legally married I couldn't encourage him any further than the friendship we enjoyed. Really enjoyed, too! But now... everything's on hold right now. I can't even think of–"

"But you are staying here in Edgemont, right?"

"Oh yes, Edgemont is my home now."

Judith squeezes Lila's hand tightly.

"I know you're really tired and, frankly, I'm pretty drained myself so we're going to take you straight home. Before coming to the airport we stopped and picked up a few perishables, you know: milk, eggs, bread, so we'll carry everything inside and then leave you to get some sleep. Are you back at school tomorrow?"

"I'm planning to go."

Grant calls out that he's reached the Edgemont exit from the highway and he needs directions to Lila's place. She starts by giving him her address and he asks:

"Do you a fire station on your street? the only one that takes back hazardous household materials?"

"Yes, do you know it?"

"I've been there. Okay, I know where I'm going now. Carry on, Judith."

"I will. As I was saying, I've got a follow-up visit at the hospital in the morning but this time it should just be a standard check and remove the bandage so I expect I'll be at school for the afternoon. But I'm going to call Pat and let her know that you'll probably be late and I'm 100% certain that will be fine, Lila. You're entitled to bereavement days anyways. So sleep as long as you can."

Tears welled up again in Lila's eyes, this time over the kindness of her friends.

Chapter Thirty-Seven

Monday, March 2, 2020

Judith's hospital visit is a speedy affair so she is back at her desk mid-morning and Lila hasn't arrived yet. Judith checks in with Pat and confirms she feels well enough to return to work.

"Your bruises have faded but one still looks particularly nasty. I see they've removed the dressing."

"Yes, and the swelling has gone down in the back of my head and on Wednesday I can actually wash my hair! because I'll have waited the full ten days by then. What a relief that's going to be. This dry shampoo makes my scalp so itchy!"

"Why not skip the shampoo and wear a headscarf or a cute beret instead? Oh well, it's your decision. The students are pleased to have everyone back as well. They get unsettled when there are *goings-on*. "

"You've got a school full of drama queens, that's why!"

"True enough. They've made you a *Get Well Soon* card and a *Sorry For Your Loss* card for Lila. The whole school has signed them."

"Even Marta?"

"Okay, *almost* the whole school has signed them!" laughs Pat.

Marta Smith is the school's oldest teacher and the years have turned her into a bitter woman filled with spite and malicious gossip. Pat Johnson would love to end her contract but no one can complain about the quality of Marta's teaching.

" I'm so glad Beth Penner has taken Margaret Seely under her wing. Beth has become such a popular girl and everyone likes her so, by extension, they're now all being good with Margaret. Once the story started circulating about her mother, and Rev Robbie and the gambling, she could easily have become a target for bullies."

"On the other hand Margaret has shown that she's a fighter. Literally!"

"Let's hope there's no more of that. I'd like to get through the next four months of this school year without any more incidents or fussing or fighting."

"Amen to that," Judith agrees.

"Although..."

"What?"

"Well, what have you been hearing about this deadly Coronavirus? this Covid-19?"

"That's only a problem in China, right? I mean, at the end of December I read about an article in... let me think.. The Washington Post, I believe, stating that Chinese news agencies had just announced a pneumonia outbreak but there was speculation that it was much more than pneumonia. That is was some sort of respiratory disease, and highly infectious."

"And of course all the cruise ships."

"I heard something but, between Lila and Grant and Rev Robbie's murder, I've been pretty distracted and wrapped up in my own issues. What's the scoop on the cruise ships?"

"One of the Princess cruise ships has been quarantined in Japan for almost a month and they've had some deaths. Other cruise ships have had outbreaks too. In 2017 Mark and I took a Caribbean cruise, remember? and we really enjoyed it, but you are in awfully close proximity with all the other passengers and crew so I can easily understand how a virus could spread quickly."

"I guess, but they've contained it, right?"

"We haven't closed our borders so I suppose it's possible that travellers and returning citizens could bring infection with them... do you recall the SARS scare back about fifteen years ago? I bet Lila remembers it, even though she'd just have been in her teens. It was a big deal in Toronto, a few dozen died and businesses had to close. There were quarantine restrictions and everything."

"I remember now that you've mentioned it, but the whole thing just kind of fizzled out, didn't it? I mean I never heard of them finding a cure but the panicking just stopped."

"Oh I know exactly what you mean, I made the same comment to Mark afterwards and he told me it stopped because of something called 'herd immunity'. I'm sure Lila can explain this better but apparently when this herd immunity happens the disease dies off or something."

"That's a clear enough explanation, Principal Johnson," says Lila smiling from the doorway.

"Lila!" Pat hurries over to give the younger woman a hug. Judith is beaming with everyone being together and she's happy although she can't miss Lila's underlying sadness.

Samira hovers in the doorway announcing she has paperwork for both Judith and Lila to sign so the reunion breaks up and they follow the secretary back to her desk in the front.

Walking back to their respective offices the two women are welcomed with plenty of well-wishing greetings, and given their respective cards.

Chapter Thirty-Eight

The week ends on an unhappy note when Pat calls Judith at home Friday night to say Mark has tested positive for Covid-19 that day, so both he and she are in quarantine. She asks Judith to again step in as Acting Principal until they get the all-clear from Alberta Health Services.

"Is Mark very sick? and do you have it too?"

"Mark said it feels like he's got the 24-hour flu. The only reason he got tested is because the hospital admitted someone who later tested positive so then they tested all personnel – staff and volunteers. I don't feel in the least bit sick but we have to isolate for the ten or fourteen day period – we're waiting to hear back for more information."

"I'll get some groceries for you and any other shopping you need–"

"Thanks, but you can't. We aren't allowed to have contact with anybody. There are some volunteer services with people all fitted up with *Personal Protective Equipment* looking after stuff like groceries and medicines – again, we're waiting for more details – but thanks so much for thinking of us, Judith. I'll definitely let you know what's going on. Luckily I'm the type of shopper who stockpiles when things are on sale so we're well-set for canned, packaged, and frozen foods plus non-food items, too."

"Thank goodness. What a thing to happen! and all because Mark generously volunteers his time to help people who are sick."

"I'm just sorry to stick you with covering my job again so soon after the last time."

"At least there's no murder mystery to solve!"

"That reminds me... I've been meaning to ask how things are going with you and the handsome detective? Now that I've got all this free time I can indulge in a gossip session with you so tell me all... are you in love?"

"Pat! I can't tell you that before I tell him."

"Oooh Judith, you are in love! Why haven't you told him?"

"Because Grant has to say the words first."

Don't miss out!

Visit the website below and you can sign up to receive emails whenever Della North publishes a new book. There's no charge and no obligation.

https://books2read.com/r/B-A-RNHX-CXYIC

BOOKS 2 READ

Connecting independent readers to independent writers.

Also by Della North

Village of Edgemont
A Deadly December in Edgemont
A Fatal February in Edgemont
A Sinister Spring in Edgemont

Watch for more at dellanorth.ca.

About the Author

Della enjoys mysteries that won't keep her up at night, have a hint of romance, and a satisfactory ending. Preferably in a series.

She and her partner live with a tuxedo cat in the sunniest city in Canada, nestled in the foothills of the Rocky Mountains.

In November of 2022 Della undertook the National Novel Writing challenge to complete a 50.000 word first draft and the Village of Edgemont series began.

Books in this series:

1 - "**A Deadly December in Edgemont**"

2 - "**A Fatal February in Edgemont**"

3 - "**A Sinister Spring in Edgemont**"

A portion of sale proceeds will be donated to NaNoWriMo.org in appreciation.

Read more at dellanorth.ca.